Flye on the Wall

by Mariah Burne

Kingman Row Entertainment, LLC

www.kingmanrow.com

Johnston, Iowa

Published by Kingman Row Entertainment, LLC.
For information, please contact:
Kingman Row Entertainment, LLC
5874 Merle Hay Road, #1159
Johnston, IA 50131
515-321-1507
Website: www.kingmanrow.com
Email: james@kingmanrow.com

First (electronic) edition, 2014.
Second (paperback) edition, 2015.
ISBN 10: 0-9960746-1-9
ISBN 13: 978-0-9960746-1-2
Library of Congress Control Number: 2014938403

Cover design by Erin Tracy.
Edited by Madhu Koduvalli and Colin Lacy.
Production coordinated by Madhu Koduvalli.

For Tom and Ryan

Chapter One

The gates of Hell gape before me and I'm being swept along with a mass of humanity accompanied by a cacophony of sound. I hold my breath as my feet leave the floor for an instant as a sharp elbow jabs me in the ribs. Head whirling, I try to shield myself against the fray as it charges into the narrow hallway that opens into a wider foyer. A blast of air conditioning hits me in my face and I can finally breathe again.

It's the first day of school at New Hope High, an uppity prep school just outside of Spring Valley, North Carolina. I'm not supposed to be here, but because I'm so freakin' brilliant, my parents thought I wasn't being challenged enough in my middle school, so I skipped eighth grade and here I am, a freshman going to school with kids who will be turning fifteen next month when I turned thirteen last week. Everything about this sucks:

I'll be the last one to drive, the last one to date. I'll be a skinny, flat-chested redhead, walking to school until I graduate when I'm sixteen. I'm gonna die.

"Jordan! Jordan!" A tall, blond girl holding a volley ball uniform, is screaming next to my ear. Her well-muscled arm crunches hard on my shoulder.

I yelp, mostly out of shock, but it hurts, too. She gives me a sidelong glance and, seeing the panic and fear on my face, decides that I'm not worth a second look, let alone an apology.

"Jordan! Jordan!" This girl is not giving up.

A few feet ahead, a slender girl wearing a cheerleader's uniform and honey-brown hair turns in irritation. She looks like a young Angelina Jolie, only prettier, if that's possible.

"For God's sake, Maddie! What?!"

Maddie elbows her way through the crowd until she's behind Jordan, embracing her in an all-encompassing hug while jumping up and down maniacally. She obviously needs to be on medication.

Jordan turns, her frown morphing into a so-happy-to-see you smile, and hugs her back. A tall, dark-haired boy tiptoes up behind Maddie and tugs on her ponytail, as though she's his personal pull toy. She whips around, quick anger flashing in her blue eyes, but when she sees who it is, she immediately squeals, "Matt!" and proceeds to mount him with her legs firmly around his waist. She gives him a big, juicy kiss.

"Get a room," someone yells from the back, accompanied by mostly friendly laughter.

Matt flips off the room in general, grinning a vacant, harmless smile, and yells back, "We're in a room!"

Aren't there any teachers here? The chaos continues, and just as I feel my breath leaving my body permanently, a strong hand firmly pulls my left arm. I'm being propelled toward the lockers, with no effort on my part. How is this happening? I don't think my feet are even touching the floor. It's a little like flying.

When I'm safely deposited at my locker in the locker bay, I look around to thank my rescuer, but all I see is a slender African-American man with graying hair under a ball cap, dressed in khakis and a knit shirt, walking away from me. He turns around and his warm, brown eyes twinkle against his dark brown skin as he lifts a finger to his lips and disappears around a corner.

I don't have time to think; the second wave is on its way. A hundred new freshmen are racing towards me. I open my locker door, thinking I can beat the crowd, only to find that it's stuck. Of course it is. What other clichéd high school trauma-dramas will I have to endure? I keep pulling on the door as the chatter about what-did-you-do-this-summer swirls around me in the open area. The kids talking over, under, around, and through their lockers are a constant reminder that I don't belong here.

"Yo, Dusty! How was tennis camp? Did you finally learn to use your racket?"

"Enough to beat your ass, man."

"Leila!"

"Jordan!"

"Cammie!"

"We made the JV squad!" Three girls in cheerleader uniforms scream, hug and high five, gathering around Maddie.

"How was Italy?"

"Oh, you know, hot and boring. It's like one giant museum. But I did get some really cute shoes."

"Oh my God. Bruno Maglis!" The cheerleaders squeal as Maddie lifts her left leg, steadying herself on her locker door. "Those Italian guys are so hot. And they love American blondes."

Spring Valley is an upwardly-mobile, not-quite-suburb of Durham and Chapel Hill. There's some ethnic diversity here, but almost everyone is at least upper middle class. Even in middle school, it wasn't unusual for kids to go to the Turks and Caicos for spring break, or go skiing in Switzerland for winter break.

Some of these kids look vaguely familiar from my old middle school, but since they were a grade ahead of me and I didn't associate with them then (their choice, not mine), it doesn't seem likely that that's going to change now. No one talks to me, but I'm getting some glances and smirks as I continue to struggle with my locker door. Thank God I don't have a lock to deal with. Hot tears threaten at the corners of my eyes and I blink them away furtively, knowing that my life will only get worse if I let these kids see me cry. Obviously they already think I'm a baby. Worse than a baby. I'm an embryo.

A sturdy, brown hand gently moves mine away from the door and deftly opens it.

"Shazaam!"

"Thank you!" I gasp. It's the same man who had extricated me from the crowd. My arms tingle with goose flesh. It's almost like he just materialized out of thin air.

"I'm Lester Murdock. Mr. Lester to y'all here. I look out for you, Little Flye Girl. Because that's my job. I take care of everyone here."

"How...how do you know my name?" I'm so confused right now. He laughs.

"We know all about you Little Flye Girl. We've been eagerly anticipating your arrival." He laughs again, radiating pure joy and something else. It's like he's glowing. Or, you know, I'm going crazy.

"Why? I mean, I'm really not supposed to be here. I mean I go to school here, but I'm not old enough..." *I sound like an extra-stupid fourth grader.*

"You'll be just fine. Anything else I can do for you?"

I might as well ask, since I already sound like an idiot. "Um, well, if you could tell me where my first class is?"

He looks at my schedule and points me towards the English room before he walks away again. But then he turns suddenly, points a finger at me and says with a grave smile, "Remember, Little Flye Girl, wherever you are is exactly where you're supposed to be."

Chapter Two

The bell is ringing as I take a seat in the back of the room. Taking out a notebook and pen, I glance around the room and notice that some of the cheerleaders and guys from the lockers are sitting on the far side of the room, near the front, still talking and laughing.

My side of the room is mainly occupied by kids who are dressed like me, in jeans, T-shirts with computer logos or gaming graphics, and sneakers. Most of us sport glasses and un-styled (or uncombed) hair. Some of these kids have braces, and most of the girls are not wearing makeup. I've only been in high school for fifteen minutes and the caste system is already clear. At least I chose the right side of the room.

I turn my attention to the front as the teacher calls out, "Good morning!" A few people greet her; most just stop talking and look at her. She's small, with long, curly gray hair and big, brown eyes, and she's wearing at least five pounds of necklaces and bracelets. She looks like an old hippie. Not the pseudo-hip image my parents try to portray with their tie-dyed shirts, sandals, and hybrid car, but the real thing, like she probably got some of that jewelry at Woodstock. "Mrs. Meercamp" is written on the board.

She starts taking attendance and eventually gets to me. "Flye Shannahan."

There are some titters and eye rolling from the cheering section of the room. Mrs. Meercamp quickly snaps, "That's enough!" She makes eye contact with each of the offending students until the room is quiet. She smiles at me.

"Flye. That's an unusual name. I, for one, love unusual names." She continues, drawing in the rest of the class. "Like Titus Andronicus. And Mercutio and Portia. Anyone familiar with those names?"

I see blank faces on most of the kids. I keep my eyes on my desk. I know those names. I read some of Shakespeare's tragedies this summer for fun. I see Matt whispering and quietly laughing with a guy he calls Danny. Mrs. Meercamp walks between them and stands there. It only takes a few seconds for them to get quiet and look up guiltily.

"Gentlemen, I assume you're discussing Mercutio?"

Matt reddens, clears his throat, and says softly, "Uh, no ma'am, we were just saying that a Porsche is a car."

There's the sound of suppressed laughter from my side of the room and some guy fake coughs, "Stupid!"

Again, Mrs. Meercamp gives us an icy look and all is quiet. She returns her attention to Matt, trying to discern if he's being a smart ass, but on his face, there's only open sincerity and a vague certainty that he's right. She relents, smiles a little and says, "You're right, Matt."

What?!

"A Porsche is a car. A very nice one, I might add."

Several kids on the dweebish side of the room exchange looks of incredulity as she begins to write on the board:

PORSCHE = A GERMAN SPORTS CAR

PORTIA = FEMALE CHARACTERS IN
   SHAKESPEREAN PLAYS

PORTIA = MRS. MEERCAMP'S FIRST NAME (NO
   RELATION TO SHAKESPEARE) ☺

"So, in a sense, you're right. However. That's not exactly the answer I was looking for." She smiles wryly.

The general looks of boredom have morphed into looks of respect for not belittling him, and I feel it too. Mrs. Meercamp is a good teacher.

She goes on to give us our first assignment, due this Friday. "You will write an essay. Five paragraphs, no more than two typed pages. Double spaced and use twelve-point plain font. No pink curlicues, no giant letters that take up an entire page, no 'Zapf Dingbats.'

"The topic is beliefs and values. This is your first day of high school. What's important to you? Right here, right now, in this very moment, what do you value most? You can write about anything you want, but be very clear about this one thing: you have to be honest. You have to be real. The essay comes completely from you, not your parents, not your friends. You.

And," she adds wryly, "if at all possible, please don't write about world peace. This is not a pageant."

She turns on the projector to bring the writing requirements up and nothing happens. She presses keys, turns the projector off and on again, and still nothing. The class is getting restless and Mrs. Meercamp is getting flustered. I get up and go over to her, seeing if there's something I can do to help.

It's simple. I right click on the monitor screen, click on "Graphics Options" and change the option to "Monitor Plus Screen." *Voila!* She's good to go. I sit back down in my seat to some appreciative looks from my side of the room and a few snickers from the other side.

"Good job, Flye. Thank you so much." Mrs. Meercamp moves over to the computer cart and starts checking out laptops.

It was nothing, really. At computer camp this summer, there was this guy, Steven, who was basically a computer genius. He bragged once that he had hacked into the CIA's computers. I didn't really believe him, but we were pretty competitive with each other and I learned a lot from him.

I check out a laptop and begin to write furiously. "I believe I shouldn't be here. It doesn't matter that my IQ rang in somewhere around 165. It doesn't matter that I started to talk at seven months of age and was speaking in complete sentences by the time I was two. It doesn't matter that I learned to read when I was three. None of this matters because I SHOULDN'T BE HERE!!!!!!!"

Then I highlight everything and hit the backspace key before Mrs. Meercamp can read it over my shoulder. I watch her walk around the room, talking to kids here and there, kneeling down to see their computer screens, asking questions, smiling and laughing occasionally as she gets to know the kids better.

I try again. "I believe that grade skipping is a finely tuned weapon of self-destruction, beside which drinking, doing drugs, and cutting appear to be healthy emotional choices. I'm here because I have an intellectual snob for a mother and an absentee father who cares more about bugs in South America than he does about me." I erase it again. Oh, God. She's coming toward me. I look at my blank screen and then up at her, panicking. I should be doing better than this.

She smiles. "Are you stuck?"

I nod dumbly. Evidently I have no words at all today, written or spoken. Yep, that's me. Just an illiterate fool. So much for being brilliant.

She keeps smiling. "Don't worry about it. Just try writing down a few words that come to mind."

I write "rage," "impotent," "hopeless," and "victim," as she keeps moving around the room, helping kids here and there, actually teaching instead of just sitting at her desk and lording over us.

The bell rings and I'm released from death by writer's block. I pick up my stuff and head out the door for my next class. Behind me I hear someone say, "Yo, Matt! First right answer in high school. You're a genius, man." I glance around and see Danny high-fiving with Matt. The cheerleaders are gathered around him, simpering and flirting.

Seriously? Matt thought that Shakespeare wrote a part for a sports car into one of his plays? And they're proud of him? Oh. My. God.

Chapter Three

It's lunchtime. This is the moment I've been dreading all morning while obsessing over that age-old question: who will I sit with? I walk into the cavernous cafeteria that echoes with teenaged babble and laughter. It smells like boiling socks. I walk slowly, looking for anyone who might not leave if I sit down at their table. The cheerleaders, Matt, and some other guys are sitting at a round table, where I'll have to walk right by them.

I'm intercepted by an incredibly hot guy. I stop dead in my tracks and my tongue is stuck to the roof of my mouth just from looking at him. All he's done is step in front of me and say, "Hi," but I've got what feels like peanut butter mixed with cotton balls in my mouth, so I just stand there, staring at his amazing shaggy blond hair, iceberg blue eyes, and chiseled jawline and cheekbones.

He smirks down at me, and his eyes become even more frigid as I stand there for several seconds, saying absolutely nothing. "Hey, what's your name, ginger shrimp?" He stares at me with growing contempt and I can barely choke out, "Flye."

And he's off: "Are you a bug, ginger? I almost stepped on a fly. This kid is really bugging me. Anyone got a fly swatter? There's a fly in the cafeteria; someone call an exterminator."

It's a stand-up routine with my name, as if I haven't heard it all a million times before. Everyone is laughing; the cheerleaders are falling over in their seats, and Matt is banging his fist on the table with his head thrown back, yelling, "You rock, Chris," at my tormentor, who doesn't seem nearly as hot as he did at first glance. I seem to be the only one in the room who's aware that none of these jokes are even remotely funny.

"You know, with all that ginger hair, you should have been called a fire ant!" This is his parting burn as he sits back down to another general shout of laughter.

So what does that make you, a pissant? That would be my normal response, but the moment is over and Chris is basking in the glory of having just humiliated a total stranger. No one would hear anything I say now.

I do stand up for myself, at least sometimes, but not today when I'm standing alone and everyone in the cafeteria is laughing their ass off at me. Today I seem to be incapable of uttering anything even vaguely resembling normal human communication.

Stuffing a bottle of juice in my lunch bag, I leave and go looking for a nook where I can be alone by choice, not by general exclusion. The halls are empty and quiet, so I walk absent-mindedly down a well-lit and brightly colored hall with a gorgeous, hand-painted mural depicting North Carolina scenes of the beach, the mountains, and various sports venues. I loiter along, enjoying the mural and the silence until I come upon the rear exit. There are stairs going down, probably into the basement. I glance around and see no one, so I follow the stairs down. I walk down another hall with computer equipment, white boards, boxes of supplies and empty desks randomly shoved up against the far wall.

It's darker down here, poorly lit and a little spooky. Someone forgot to change some light bulbs. I hear something scuffling and look for a mouse or worse. There's a silhouette of a man ahead of me in the dingy light, and I recognize him: Mr. Lester. At least, I think it's him. Maybe he'll save me, if not from the crowd of crazies, then at least from myself. He turns a corner and I follow him. I find myself in yet another hall used for storage, but it's narrower and a little brighter. There's a smudge on the right-hand wall and I absently rub it with my elbow.

The walls glow faintly, with colored spots fading in and out of my peripheral vision, as if I've been staring at the sun too long. I blink and then rub my eyes. Looking down the hall, everything seems darker against the brightly lit wall. This is too weird; what's going on here? I look back at the glowing wall again and it begins to fade, and I fade too, sinking to the floor, shaking and covering my face with my sweaty hands.

There's no logical explanation for a glowing wall. I think I've just had some kind of out-of-body experience. Or I'm on an acid trip. Or maybe it was a seizure or a message from outer space. Maybe I have a brain tumor.

Oh God. What if that's it? Like that guy in that old movie my mom loves, *Phenomenon*, where he thinks he's had a close encounter with a UFO because he sees these lights that knock him out, and then he starts getting all these powers, like he can move objects by telekinesis, and he memorizes a Portuguese dictionary in an hour, and everyone's afraid of him because he breaks a mirror in a bar using only his mind, and then he finds out he has a brain tumor that's making him do all this stuff, and then everyone pities him, and he dies. And it's very sad.

Okay, Flye. Get a grip. You're getting way ahead of yourself here.

I study the wall, almost hoping that it will glow again so that I can figure it out, but it doesn't, and I'm simultaneously relieved and disappointed. I continue to gaze mindlessly at the wall, and I notice something else weird. To the left, behind a whiteboard, the wall is coming apart. I push the white board aside to get a better look, and I can see that the wall is actually a door, which is slightly ajar. I push it a little and peer into a small, empty room. It looks like someone made a mistake when the school was still under construction, and built a room, complete with a door, where there wasn't supposed to be a room. Instead of framing in the door, they tried to camouflage it as part of the wall. It would have worked beautifully if the door hadn't been left just a tad bit open.

I can't possibly stand by a wall that is actually a door without going in to see where it goes, so here I go. Through the looking glass.

The first thing I notice is the lack of an otherworldly glow, which is a relief. This is just an empty area, with holes cut in the walls for air vents, power outlets, whatever, without any grating on them. The ceiling is really high, and there must be a window up there somewhere, because there's soft daylight filtering down.

There's a thin layer of dust on the floor and it's warm and cozy in here, probably because it's so small—about the size of my closet. I'm still reeling from my hallucination/seizure/whatever, but I feel oddly safe in this little room, so I look around some more.

The door has a knob and lock on this side. I think that this was meant to be some kind of utilities room, but someone got the dimensions wrong, so they just tried to gloss it over by making the room look like it wasn't there. Well, maybe not, but I can wrap my head around this explanation more readily than I can, "Hey, I just found a portal to cosmic dimensions in my school's basement."

The residual effects of my adrenaline rush are completely gone, vanishing in light of this new discovery. Hmm. I think I just found my own little private cafeteria. I can bring my lunch in here, lock the door behind me, and have an hour of uninterrupted blissful quiet to myself. I can read in here, do homework, bring a sketchbook. The possibilities are endless. I can just be me for a little while each day.

When I leave, I close the door almost completely behind me, and pull the whiteboard back to its original place, so that no one can see the door in the wall. It's surprising that no one has found the room yet, but I'm sure that if any of the other students knew about it, there would be cigarette butts or a bong or something equally disgusting down here. I touch the wall again, but no lights appear. Sighing and shrugging my shoulders, I walk carefully back upstairs, making sure no one sees me.

As I turn the corner to walk back down the hall toward my locker, a slight motion catches my peripheral vision to my right. Mr. Lester is leaning against the wall facing the basement stairs.

His eyes are sparkling and knowing as he catches my gaze. He silently tips his cap and glides away like a cat.

Chapter Four

Brrring! The end-of-lunch bell is ringing as I slam my locker shut and power walk to my next class, Ancient History. I take a right, walk to the end, and there it is on the right. The teacher is standing at the front of the room, shooting the breeze with a group of kids I haven't seen in my other classes before. They must be sophomores. I take a seat in the middle of a row off to the side, next to a girl I recognize from Geometry. Her brown hair is in braids, and she's wearing skinny jeans with a purple tank top under a green cami, a style I think of as "eclectic prep." She smiles at me and says, "Hey."

I smile back, and watch the teacher who's working the room, calling out to kids and generally making himself the center of attention.

"Yo, Josh. How's it going? Jazzy, Kayla, Beth." He nods to each one, making his jowls jiggle. "Did y'all have a good summer?"

The girls all smile and nod, finding places to sit by the wall across from me, next to Danny and Matt. They whisper something to a pretty, black-haired, brown-skinned girl in the group, who giggles and whispers back. They were all sitting together when Chris destroyed me at lunch; I slump in my seat, lower my head, and pull my hair around my face.

"Hey, y'all. I'm Mr. Schwartz and this is Ancient History. If you're not supposed to be in here, there's the door. Good luck with finding your next class."

There are a few grins, but no one leaves. He passes around a seating chart for people to sign in.

"Welcome back, sophomores. Welcome to high school, freshmen – Yo, Nico. Hey, Peter. How's it going? Steph, get your license yet?" Then, as he looks around the room with a big grin on his face: "Consider yourselves warned, guys. She's out on the roads now."

A few kids smile and the girl rolls her eyes, blushing slightly.

"Okay, okay, let's get started, but first, a history joke." The sophomores groan; the freshmen look confused.

"I wish I had been born a thousand years ago. Now someone ask me why."

"Why?"

"Just think of all the history that I wouldn't have to learn!"

Almost everyone cracks up, except me. This is stupid. Is he going to teach anything or is he just going to keep bullshitting around? A couple of other kids and I make eye contact. We're thinking the same thing: *Who is this clown?*

A few kids in the front are hanging on every word. There's always some in every class: the kids who suck up to every teacher. The rest of the class is ready for another joke. I don't like this guy. Okay, so I know I'm not being fair, but he's just trying too hard, acting like he's another kid instead of the adult unit in the room. He's bowing and smiling, like a talk show host, getting the crowd settled down. Now he's pulling up a slide presentation from which he begins to read, verbatim.

Well, thank God for that. It's not like I already know how to read or anything. *Stop it, Flye! What's the matter with you? You usually give people a chance, and now you're starting to act like the jerks that treat you like crap.*

Okay, okay. I'm in a really shitty mood after everything that happened at lunch, and I'm just taking it out on Schwartz. I'll try harder.

"Miss Carlson, could you please give us the definition of 'ancient' as it applies to history?"

Yeah, never mind. This guy sucks.

It looks like he's one of those teachers who just calls out names without waiting for anyone to raise their hand. I hate it when they put you on the spot like that; it never proves anything, and it's just embarrassing if you get the answer wrong.

"Miss Carlson" is a sweet looking girl behind me in a pink sweater set and dangly sand dollar earrings, with "Jody" written in purple bubble letters on her notebook. She blushes bright red and whispers, "Uh, really, really old?"

There are some giggles around the room and, instead of quieting the hecklers, Mr. Schwartz grins, showing a row of dingy teeth that could use some bleaching. He seems ready to join them in laughing at her. He bounces up and down on the balls of his feet, and I wonder if he's doing that to make himself look taller. It's not working. He consults the seating chart and picks another name at random.

"Mr. Robertson? How about you? Can you give us the definition of 'ancient'?"

The tall, lanky kid in the back starts awake. "Do what now?"

More giggles and Schwartz sighs audibly and shakes his head melodramatically, looking over at the cool kids' section as if to say, "You see what I have to deal with?"

Alright. Enough. I raise my hand. "Yes? Miss...uh..." He combs his bushy beard with his fingers, searching the seating chart.

"Shannahan. Flye Shannahan. I think Jody's definition is a good one, but I think you should include oral history, like the ancient storyteller by the fire. Because that gives us our history today. Ancient history was a bunch of cave dwellers telling stories that filtered down through generations. I mean, we still read ancient stories like *Beowulf* and *Tristan and Isolde*. So, that's what 'ancient' means."

Okay, so I'm smart. I usually don't show off like that, but sometimes I can't resist, especially when the teacher is a douche bag who targets people in class for kicks. It takes a while for Schwartz to pull his jaw up off the floor.

The girl next to me whispers, "Wow, nice save. Jody's just really shy and Schwartz just, like, picks on her all the time. It's like he sucks up to the popular kids and just totally terrorizes the others. My sister had him and she says he does this all the time."

I glance at Schwartz, but he's busy targeting his next victim. "Yeah, I got that gross-teacher vibe from him."

"Most of us call him 'Gimli' 'cause he looks like the dwarf from *The Lord of the Rings*."

I can't help it; I grin. "Oh my God, that's way too perfect."

"Yeah, I mean, he's got the little arms and the big head and everything."

I laugh quietly in agreement.

"I'm Jennifer. Jenn."

"I'm Flye."

"Yeah, I know. Word gets around fast here. Are you really twelve?"

"No." I go to explain my unique peculiarities, but Gimli's rotund shadow falls upon us before I can start.

"Excuuuuuuse me, Miss Shannahan, Miss Shaw. Is there a problem?" Schwartz drawls out his question, riddled with sarcasm, beaming his shiny, avian eyes on us. I freeze. I've never been called down in class before.

"Not at all, sir. Sorry, sir," Jenn says quickly and smiles at me. I smile back.

"Right. Turn to the first page of your textbook and talk about the table of contents." He gives us one last frigid glance and then grins at the popular side of the room again.

There are a few quiet sighs and groans but everyone obediently opens the book to the table of contents. I surreptitiously insert *The Catcher in the Rye*, glancing around the room to make sure no one sees me.

At the end of the day, I grab my books out of my locker, stuff my backpack full and tie my jacket around my waist. The day's over and I'm still alive. Overall, it went better than I had expected. Finding an opening in the crowd, I get lost in it, just another lemming. I make my way out the front door and head towards home.

Chapter Five

"Hello, Flye," the girl in front of me simpers. She's pretty, but she would be drop-dead gorgeous if she'd take off some of her makeup and stop dressing like a wannabe hooker. Her brown eyes are rimmed with heavy eyeliner and one of her fake eyelashes is coming loose at the corner. It's hilarious, but she'd probably freak at this disastrous fashion malfunction. I bite my tongue and stay silent. Her long, dark hair is halfway down her back, and I smell her powder-pink lip gloss: strawberry. She's got that sweet-trashy look that the other girls in her group try so hard to cultivate. These are the popular girls who've had me in their sights all day, and now they've cornered me on the sidewalk, away from the prying eyes of supervisory-type adults. These girls are the Inner Circle. I usually call them The Belles. They circle me like a pack of coyotes.

I think of these girls as the kind of people who list "power shopping" as an extracurricular activity on their college applications, who were born knowing how to lead boys around like pet puppies, who were baptized in the same gene pool as their mamas, who are still the belles of the country club. There are about fifteen of them, arranged in order of rank, with a few satellites orbiting the periphery.

She's holding my gaze, but I continue to say nothing. I'm in war mode and I know that this is not the Queen Bee—the Chief Belle. This is one of her lieutenants, scoping out the new girl. How do I know? Been here, done this.

"My name is Leah. You are called Flye, aren't you? Is that your real name?" She's pressing for an answer. She's still sweet, dripping sugar and smiling, but her eyes are narrow, judging and hard.

I finally nod. *You already know that. Ask me something you don't know.*

She drops the sweet act and oozes insolence. "Are you shy? A shy Flye. Isn't that sweet?" She turns to the rest of the girls and says, "She's just a shy little girl!" There's laughter from the group and I see Jenn from ancient history on the edge of the group whisper something to a guy next to her. They walk away, unnoticed by the others. I recognize some of the girls from class: Jazzy, Maddie, Jordan. That hot asshole, Chris, from the cafeteria, and his buddies are also standing by, listening and grinning. They're the boy equivalent of the Belles. I call them the Jokes. (My word-play on "Jocks.") Everyone's watching this little drama unfold with bright, predatory interest.

Another girl joins us. This is the Queen. She's tall, slender, and blond with bright green eyes, which look like a rich, well-fertilized lawn. Must be tinted contacts. No act of nature ever created eyes that color in a human being, although I've seen them on certain reptiles. She looks me up and down, dismissively, and says, "Well, darlin', look what just flew in. Flye. What an interestin' name. However did y'all end up with a name like that?" Her voice is soft and overtly Southern. Scarlet O'Hara would be proud.

I say nothing. She doesn't want me to speak. She's just showing off my total lack of status to her audience. I now have a target on my back, and everyone knows about it.

The Queen looks down at me, dripping arrogance and contempt. She inspects her perfect French manicure and then stares at me. "I'm Emily. Just for future reference. Not that you'll ever be talking to me." She turns back to her crowd, laughing, and everyone joins in. It's basically a reprise of the cafeteria at lunch.

I put on my best I-couldn't-give-a-rat's-ass-about-you look, turn on my heel and walk away without a word. A string of biting remarks follows me: "Go back to grade school!"

"Are you allowed to cross the street alone?"

"Nice t-shirt! My little sister has one just like it!"

A chorus of raucous laughter follows me across the street. Do they really think it's funny, or are they all so programmed to follow the leader that they don't even think? Just act and react?

I glance back over my shoulder, out of curiosity or self-protection, I'm not sure which, as Jordan calls out a final question. "Do you even wear a bra?"

Then they're off to their next victim, closing in on a tall, skinny kid with dark hair in his eyes, walking in the posture of the terminal dweeb: head down, shoulders slumped, eyes focused straight ahead, trying to be invisible. "Hey Jake. How's it going, man?" says Chris as he purposefully walks into the poor kid. Jake stumbles and falls to one knee, and Chris holds out a hand to help him up, saying, "Oh, sorry, man, my fault." He pulls too hard so that the kid stumbles yet again on the sidewalk. It's all as well-rehearsed as a practiced football play, and Jake doesn't even bother to look up as he gets to his feet again and shrugs, ignoring their leers. He's used to it all. His eyes meet mine for just a second and then he nods at me. One grunt in the war acknowledging another. I nod back and try to smile, but I think it comes out more like a grimace.

I turn and walk away. This time I make it home.

Chapter Six

I flop on my bed and plug into some Simon and Garfunkel. The theme from *Bookends* plays as I gaze out my window, watching the moon that's barely visible against the still-blue sky. I've had this affinity for the moon since I was little. It's like my talisman; I watch it in its monthly cycles, waxing and waning, feeling the rhythm of the earth and the turning of the seasons. It keeps me grounded, especially that first silver sliver each month, so young and hopeful, like I used to be. My throat aches and threatens to close up as tears roll down my face, and I let them, giving in to all the fear, frustration, anger, and pain that's all that's left of me after this day from Hell.

A montage of grotesquely distorted images floats before my closed eyes, and I see myself, damp and frazzled, struggling with my stupid locker door; Chris leering at me in the cafeteria with all the Belles and the Jokes roaring in laughter; Mr. Schwartz laughing his fat ass off at anyone he can; and Leah and Emily howling like feral cats while I'm clutching a math book against my pathetic, shapeless t-shirt, their mouths morphing into gigantic, distorted, red lips overlapping monstrous, bleached teeth. I hear someone sobbing out of control and realize that it's me.

Another image floats into my head: the glowing psychedelic walls pulsing and breathing, and the warm, quiet space of my secret room where no one can ever find me. My breathing slows, and my tears recede as I allow myself to be drawn into this memory of my little room, where I can get some perspective on my new high school life, and decide how I'm going to survive the next 180 days.

Today was certainly not my first encounter with girls like Emily and her crowd. They've been a part of my life since fifth grade when Cecilia Post moved to my school. She had long, straight hair, pretty clothes, and breasts. One day in the bathroom after recess, I watched her give me the once over, taking in my tangled mess of red hair, my right sock that had slumped its way halfway into my sneaker, my glasses that were slipping down my sweaty nose, and my braces that probably had a piece of broccoli stuck in them, as a look of combined dislike, amusement, and contempt came over her face. No one had ever looked at me like that before.

Cecilia quickly became the most popular girl in our class. Most of the other girls imitated her style, her hair, her handwriting, her every move. Most of the boys just hung around her and her Belles with their tongues hanging out, hoping that she would at least glance at them. I ignored her, since she clearly didn't want to be around me, and hung out with Rebekkah and Julia, who had been my friends practically since birth.

The first time it happened, I didn't know how to react. It was a lovely spring day: dogwoods and azaleas were blooming, and the sky was Carolina blue. I was just walking down the sidewalk outside of school with my friends, when Cecilia and her girls met us face to face. They looked like they were ready for a showdown. Then, as if on some silent cue, they all screamed and ran away. It was pretty weird, but then one of them turned around and yelled, "Come on, chase us! You wimps can't catch us!"

We were little kids and didn't really have any street smarts, so we ran after them. This became a regular occurrence, a strange game in which I chased after girls whom I had no chance of catching, as they laughed and called me names. I was hoping that chasing girls who despised me might be a way that I could earn my way into their group. I was young and naïve and didn't understand games.

One day, as I was beginning the chase, one of the bigger girls flew at me from out of nowhere, landing me on the ground flat on my stomach, knocking the air out of me. I couldn't breathe. I was terrified—I didn't know what was happening, and I thought I would die. She continued to sit on me, rubbing my face in the dirt, breathing hard and laughing, until they finally all ran away. I made my way into the girls' bathroom where Rebekkah helped me clean up, and then we went to tell our teacher. I was sure everything would be alright.

I was wrong. My teacher was nice, but she asked so many questions, that by the time we were done talking, I had a vague feeling that I had somehow done something to deserve what I got. Parents were called, and meetings were held. The girls apologized, even though they didn't really mean it; they were just sorry they got caught. Most of the parents were horrified, but not Cecilia's. They said their darlin' girl could never do such a thing, and that someone must have provoked her beyond her control. Meaning me. The girls backed off, and things did change.

But they also stayed the same. Fifth grade ended, and Cecelia and the Belles started middle school in a different homeroom than mine. They stayed away from me, and when they started hanging out at the mall and having boy-girl parties, I wasn't invited.

Mom and Dad said those girls were mean to me because they were jealous that I was so much smarter than they were, which made no sense to me. I knew what I looked like; I had nothing for them to be jealous of. But that's when I stopped answering so many questions in class, when I started sneaking books into class to read. Groups started fissioning off, like so many mini-nuclear reactions, into the Belles and the Jokes, the artsy-fartsy crowd, the boarders, the computer geniuses, the druggies, the church group, and Rebekkah, Julia, and me. We were the leftovers.

Rebekkah moved away when her dad got transferred to another state, and Julia was absorbed into the outer edges of the Belles. I learned to live alone, inside my head, making up a world in which I was the star; a world with no fear, no pain, no shame. The world of the lone wolf, waiting to find my pack.

Chapter Seven

The first thing I see are the Belles and the Jokes hanging out around my locker. Maddie and Leila smile sweetly and chorus at me: "Hey, Flye." I'm so caught off guard that I smile back and say, "Hey," as I swing open my locker to take out stuff for English. A huge purple bra hangs inches in front of my face, swaying slightly. My hand recoils, and I gasp involuntarily; I can feel the flush start to take over my face. The bra's cups are padded and look like bumpers on an old Buick. It's a size 46DD. There's a note attached: "Welcome to New Hope High—a place to grow."

An explosion of laugher surrounds me as I stumble, both literally and figuratively. What I should really say is, "Emily, I think you lost this," and toss it to her. Or throw it to Chris, who's practically drooling on Emily, and say, "Here, wanna practice with this?"

But I'd rather die of embarrassment than stoop to their level, so I just leave the monstrosity hanging there. As I get my books and walk away, I notice that Chris has caught the entire scene on his cell phone. Great. Now my humiliation will be all over the Internet.

Walking into English, I take a laptop from the cart by the door, sit down at my desk and start to write, the words flowing out the tips of my fingers.

"We live in an age of conformity, where being a sheep is not only preferred but expected, rather than being a lone wolf. A sheep is never alone. A sheep is always accepted, always has friends, always feels safe, and never really has to think for itself."

"A lone wolf is, by definition, alone. A lone wolf lives on the edge of the crowd, observing and following her own instincts, his own intellect, her own heart. Henry David Thoreau was a lone wolf. So were Mahatma Gandhi and Eleanor Roosevelt. A sheep usually thinks that a lone wolf is its enemy. Not so. A lone wolf is a sheep's best teacher."

I'm suddenly aware of Mrs. Meercamp reading over my shoulder with a look of thoughtful surprise on her face. Our eyes meet, and she says, "Nice. Very nice. What else do you have in there?"

She lightly taps the top of my head and turns to another kid, and I blink with surprise when I recognize who it is. It's Jake, the kid who was tripped by the Jokes after school yesterday. I watch him from the corner of my eye, noticing how he slumps in his chair, his eyes focused directly on his blank computer screen, barely acknowledging Mrs. Meercamp's existence. His long, black hair falls across his eyes and his pale cheeks, and his mouth is set in a firm, flat line. He's trying to not care, but his mouth gives him away: a full, long lower lip with a shorter upper lip that makes him look young and vulnerable, like a little boy trying to look like a grownup. He's actually kind of cute in a disaffected, defeated sort of way.

I keep covertly glancing at him until he catches my eye and smiles. "Hey, I'm Jake. Saw what those assholes were doing to you yesterday."

"Yeah, well, you too." I look around nervously, not wanting to get caught.

Mrs. Meercamp is watching us quietly, so I just turn back to my computer while still sneaking glances at Jake. Yeah, he's definitely cute, but there's something else there, too. He looks alone. Like me.

The bell rings and I make it through the rest of my morning classes. Walking down the hall to get my lunch out of my locker, I pass Leah and Maddie, who giggle, "Going to clean out your locker?" They explode in outrageous laughter as they turn into the cafeteria, and I see them pointing at me and laughing with the rest of the Belles at their table.

Mr. Schwartz is hanging out in the hall with a couple of Jokes. I hear him call them Brandon and Tyler. They're just standing there, talking and laughing. He saw the whole thing and did nothing, the douche. He's supposed to watch out for all students, not just the Belles and the Jokes. What an asshole.

"How 'bout those Heels?" I hear him ask, and that's all it takes. Brandon and Tyler are off, discussing players, stats, coaches, and rivals. From what I've noticed, these two guys are only in the Jokes' group because of their love of basketball, which is like a religion here in the south.

Gimli interrupts and says, "Yo, dudes, I've got a whole pizza and I can't eat it all. Y'all wanna come in and finish it?"

They couldn't be happier. Basketball and free pizza. What more could they want?

I notice Jake off in a corner, talking with a kid I hear him call Cody, who's wearing a heavy metal t-shirt and baggy black jeans. Cody has long, greasy, dust-colored hair and colorless eyes behind rimless glasses. His skin is pallid, and if he wasn't wearing so much black, he'd be pretty much invisible. Maybe that's what he's trying to be.

They're sitting on the floor, in a corner between two lockers, playing a video game. Gaming, like texting, is not allowed at New Hope High, but we have an honor code. That's the reason we're not allowed to have locks on our lockers. We're supposed to be more honorable than breaking into someone else's locker. Yeah, right.

Jake and Cody are talking and laughing, lost in their fantasy world, when Cody looks up sharply, fear etched into his angular features.

Mr. Lester is standing right there. I didn't see him walk up, and apparently neither did Jake and Cody. "Hey, Mr. Lester. How's it going?" Cody's face is soft and friendly, smiling politely.

"Fine, just fine. How're y'all doing?" Mr. Lester watches them carefully.

"Great, man, how're you?" They quickly put their games into their pockets.

"Guys, you know you're not supposed to use electronics in the halls."

"We know, but no one follows that rule. And besides, Cody's teaching me to play 3D chess."

"Really? I like chess too, but this looks complicated."

"Oh, it's not that hard, once you understand it," Cody says, his eyes still on his game. Then he looks up pleadingly and says, "Mr. Lester, don't get us in trouble. We'll do homework instead." He takes out a book, turns to a random page and starts to read. Jake does the same.

Mr. Lester sighs and shakes his head. "Just listen for a minute. I worry about you boys, especially you, Cody,"

"Yessir."

"Last year was hard for you, you know, with English and all that. And that must've been really hard when you're so good in math." Cody keeps his eyes on the floor and says nothing.

Mr. Lester gently bumps him with an elbow. "You understand what I'm saying?"

"Yessir."

"So what's going to be different this year?"

"I'll do better, Sir."

"I hope so. Tell me how."

"Uh, I'll go to Mr. Dickenson every day like I'm supposed to. And, uh, I won't play video games at school. And, uh, I'll do homework at night and, uh...?"

Jake picks up where Cody left off. "Me too."

"I hope so 'cause I want all my kids to do well and get along."

"Yessir, thank you, sir," they say in unison, looking at him seriously until he tips his cap, turns and walks away.

Cody sighs in resignation and says, "Man, I hate going to see Dickenson. Everyone knows I'm special ed and all they do is rag on me. Like Chris this morning. He chucked a first grade beginning-to-read book at me and then offered to help me read it. Asshole."

That sounds like the Chris I know. An equal opportunity bully. I squish into my locker even more. I feel sorry for Cody and I don't want to embarrass him further.

"Hey, man, let me see that book." Cody hands him the book

"Let me help you out, man. No one has to know." His voice is soft and compassionate as he starts quietly reading aloud.

Cody snatches it away. "For Christ sakes, Jake! You're making it worse. Anyone who sees us...they're all out to get me anyway, they're always looking at me, following me..."

He looks around the deserted area furtively and, seeing no one, pulls out his game and starts clicking the keys furiously.

"Ha! Gotcha! Check. You're in deep shit now, man."

The gross bra is still hanging there in my face, taunting me, and I stuff it into my backpack and leave silently, walking through the empty hallway toward the basement stairs and my safe little room. When I get there, I touch the painted wall lightly, just checking, but nothing happens and I'm both relieved and vaguely disappointed. The door in the wall is just as I left it, so I go in, pulling it closed behind me and pressing the lock. I sit in a corner (planning to bring something more comfortable to sit on, like a comforter), and open my lunch.

Jake and Cody look like Goths, so that sort of makes them targets for the Jokes. Cody seems to be pretty smart; he just needs a lot of extra help. But those aren't reasons for Chris and the Jokes to bully them. Why can't the Belles and the Jokes just leave everyone else alone?

Lost in my thoughts, I hear a low voice murmur off to my right. Oh my God. I'm hallucinating again, this time aurally. What *is* it with this room? I've gotta get out of here. I stand quickly, scattering carrot sticks and yogurt on the floor, and have my hand on the knob, when another voice, louder and closer to me says, "So Brittany was making out with Matt at the party?"

What?! If I'd been expecting to hear the Voice of God, this isn't what I had in mind.

"That's what Leah said. I guess they were in a bedroom when she walked in on them. But who knows? Leah was drunk off her ass and she lies about everything anyway. She's just pissed that she got dumped for you..."

And then, "Yeah, man, Coach K. is great, but no one can touch Coach Williams. They get better..."

And still more. "And five, six, seven, eight! And twirl, twirl, seven, eight and jump... Trevor, you gotta catch her before she lands on her butt..."

Oh. My. God. It's the holes in the wall. They're air vents and they're acting as conduits for sound. My entire body tingles as I realize the ramifications of this:

I can hear conversations all over the school.

All the gossip and teenage angst and who's doing what to whom. I'm on the inside looking out, for the first time in my life. I can know everything that's going on. I raise my fist in the air, and pull it down sharply, a wide grin spreading across my face. YES! Talk about karmic payback.

Well, yeah, but should I really be listening? What if I get caught? Then I'll be a bigger pariah than ever. The Belles and the Jokes will really hate me and God knows what they'll do to me then.

You won't get caught. You're smart enough to make sure that won't happen. This room was obviously meant for you, and you deserve to have it. Think about how fun it's going to be. When Emily and the Belles are giving you snark-eyes, you can laugh at them in private. You'll know all the pathetic tragedies going on in their shallow little worlds. Think how you could bare their souls for everyone to see if you wanted to. And they'd have no idea what you know. Talk about power! Isn't about time you had some?

Well, yeah. But I don't know...it doesn't seem right.

Oh for God's sake! Stop being so morally self-righteous and get a life! You can always stop if you want to.

Okay, okay, you're right. I can handle this. And I can always stop. Right? Oh man, my life just got like a million times better.

I turn my attention back to the vents and hear laughter. Someone's in the middle of a sentence. "...and did you see the look on her face when she opened her locker? Sugah, I 'bout fell over laughin'."

"Darlin', you're just so smart. It was brilliant, just brilliant."

"What's with all these losers anyway? Really. Don't we have enough already? Now we have to bring them here early from middle school? Pretty soon our group will be...a minority." The word minority comes out in a dramatic gasp, and I can't help but smile incredulously. Is this even real right now?

"I didn't think of that. You're right, we need to start a petition..."

I laugh out loud and then stuff a hand against my mouth, stricken by what I may have done. What if sound travels both ways through these vents and these girls can hear me laughing my ass off?

I freeze and listen for any sign that they heard me, but there's no reaction from them. I'm safe.

They're talking about me, laughing at me, but suddenly I don't feel as bad about it. The absolute ridiculousness of how they sound, and this sense of ultimate power combines like a chemical formula, and I'm filled with wicked joy. They can laugh all they want now, because I know everything that's happening in the school. I know more than they do. I start hearing other bits and pieces of conversations, coming from the other openings, all at once.

"We have a test tomorrow? Oh my God—"

"So then what did he say after—?"

"I just can't do this anymore, it's too hard—"

"So is Emily mad at me?"

"My parents are gone this weekend. Let's partay!"

"Homecoming's just a few weeks away. Who are you going with?"

"I hope Ramon. Can you find out for me?"

"Yeah, sure but we need to start shopping—"

The bell rings. And rings and rings and rings. Apparently, voices aren't the only things that get magnified into this room. I gather up my lunch and sneak quietly out of the room, being careful not to be seen, and make my way back to my locker. Suddenly I start shaking with silent laughter. My little room opens up everything in New Hope High; all the good, all the evil, and everything in between. My personal Pandora's Box.

Chapter Eight

When I get home, I take the bra out of my backpack, shove it in the back of a drawer and pull up my wall. There's a private message from Bekkah. It's the video Chris took today with the message, "Thought you'd want to see this. What's going on? Talk to me."

I look at the video. It's pretty choppy, and a couple of heads get in the way, but there I am, standing at my locker, holding the purple bra. The camera zooms in to get a tight shot of the satin and lace, so that the bra looks like it would fit on a cow. Then the angle zooms out to get a clear shot of my face and I brace myself for the look of total humiliation that I'm surely wearing. But I'm wrong; I don't even look fazed. I look more bored and disgusted than scared. I remember how I felt all trembly, but none of that shows. I've got a pretty good game face, I realize with pride. It's already got fifty views; God knows how many more people will see it before the night is over. But I can handle it. I think.

I message Bekkah back, "Don't worry. It's not a big deal. All freshmen have stuff like this happen."

My computer bleeps and there's the same video and a message from Stoner, my brother, who's a sophomore at Vanderbilt. He's a little more direct. "What the hell's happening? This is you, isn't it? Do I need to come down there and beat the shit outta those assholes?"

Stoner is just enough years older than me that we've never had all that sibling rivalry crap to deal with. He's very protective of me. I message him back pretty much the same thing: "Just a joke, don't worry, see you this weekend." I'll tell him everything when he gets home.

Mom comes home and wants to know all about my day. *Seriously? How much time do you have? You want to know about the locker prank? How about Mr. Schwartz, the bully who never grew up? Or—I know, you'll really love this one— let's talk about the Belles and the Jokes and their classic sense of humor.*

The version I give her is so edited that it's pretty much, "It was fine. Not much happened. How was your day?" I mean, really, what else am I going to tell her? There's nothing she can do, and it's all her fault anyway that I have to deal with all this shit. I don't owe her anything anymore.

After dinner, Mom wants to go for a walk. *Oh, yeah, right. How 'bout we just parade me around the block in a stroller while we're at it? And have the whole school come out and watch?* For someone who's supposedly so smart, Mom can be pathetically stupid.

I think fast and say, "Mom. I have a ton of homework, especially this essay for English. I don't know what to write, and it's due on Friday..."

She bites like a starving Chihuahua. "What's it on, honey? I can help."

"We're supposed to write about our beliefs and values."

"Oh wow. Mrs. Meercamp is awesome, isn't she? See, this really was the best move for you. Now you're really being challenged—"

"So, Mom, what are your beliefs?" I cut her off quickly. If she gets started on this tangent, I'll never get anything done. Besides, I don't want to listen to her lame justifications about challenges and social responsibilities. I mean, where does she think she's sending me, the Peace Corps? That would be easier.

She starts talking about human rights, individual dignity, and the sacredness of all life. There's really nothing here that I haven't heard many times before, and, to be honest, there's nothing she's saying that I don't also believe.

But then she says, "You know I'm a pacifist. I believe killing is wrong no matter what. But, see, that's just an ideal. And I used to take a lot of pride in that. But when you and Stoner were born and I held you guys and you were so tiny and needed me so much...I just felt this fierce, protective love, and I knew that if anyone ever tried to hurt either one of you, I'd kill them with my bare hands. And I'd deal with my values later."

She looks at me softly, a little teary-eyed. "But that's how I can call myself a pacifist. I choose non-violence even though I know I'm capable of cold-blooded murder."

We sit quietly for a moment, and then she says, "I don't know if that makes any sense."

"Yeah, it does. The only way to know the truth is by understanding opposites. You know, dichotomy."

She rubs her eyes and laughs softly. "I love you so much. Now go write your essay."

Chapter Nine

Walking over to my locker, I'm curiously buoyant. I feel like the last two days were a mix of the worst things that could happen, and today, with the help of my Pandora's Box, I'm going to own everything. There are a few kids hanging around the area, but no one specific is at my locker. I see Jake and Cody glance my way; Jake nods and smiles.

When I open my locker door, I almost throw up. A dozen nasty, sticky fly-strips covered in dead flies are hanging on the hooks. Some of the strips are stuck to each other, hanging so thick that I can't even put my hand in my locker without touching them. It looks like a scene from a horror film.

There's a burst of laughter behind me and I spin around, my hands shaking and my mouth gaping open. A crowd of kids are leering and grinning behind me and again, Chris is getting all of this on video.

"Ew! Someone call pest control!"

"For which fly? The ones inside the locker or the one outside?"

Please, God, don't let me cry. I scream the lyrics of *Hit Me With Your Best Shot* in my head, as a last-ditch attempt to gather my nerves and power through this hellish moment. There's a quiet cough from right next to me: Mr. Lester.

"What's going on here?"

The crowd falls silent. Mr. Lester examines the contents of my locker with a disgusted look and then addresses the group.

"I want to know who vandalized this locker."

Mr. Lester's eyes are flashing with anger as he looks around the crowd, making eye contact with each person, holding his gaze, searching for the truth. He stares at Chris for what seems like an hour until Chris begins to fidget, shuffles his feet, and stares at the floor.

Finally, Maddie's voice from the back pipes up. "We don't know. We were just walking by and wondered what all the fuss was about. We didn't do anything."

"Uh huh. I see." Mr. Lester scans the group again, which is now diminishing. "Go on to class. I'm very disappointed in whoever did this and, trust me, I will find out who it is."

He looks at Chris again, holding out his hand. "Delete the video and give me the phone."

"No way, man! This is my phone! You can't take it!" Chris's chin juts out as he folds his arms protectively across his chest, hiding the phone.

"You will delete the video and give me the phone and you will do it respectfully and politely."

He sounds like Obi-Wan Kenobi, and Chris does what he's told.

"You can get your phone from the office at the end of the day. Now go to class before you're late, because I won't give you a pass." He turns away and looks at me, worry in his eyes.

Chris turns angrily on his heel and walks away, holding his right hand behind his back and flips Mr. Lester off.

"I saw that, and I'll see you in detention." Mr. Lester hasn't taken his eyes off me.

Okay, he's got to be magic. How else could he have seen that?

"Are you alright, Little Flye Girl?"

"Yeah, I'm fine," I say, taking a shaky breath. I think I'm trying to convince myself more than I am him. "It's not a big deal."

"It *is* a big deal. Is this the first time this has happened?"

"Yes," I lie.

Ratting out the Belles and the Jokes is not going to help. I'm sure all I have to do is ride out the pranks, and they'll eventually stop out of boredom. I walk to class and lose myself with Juliet on her balcony as she falls in love with Romeo. I ignore everyone else around me.

Walking to Geometry after English, I hear buzzing sounds behind me. Fighting the urge to turn around, I walk on to class, ignoring the hecklers who are smacking their hands together, yelling, "Got it!"

A couple of girls are singing the lyrics to Miley Cyrus' *Fly on the Wall*, but it's not totally miserable. A couple of kids give me looks that seem to say, "How can they not know how stupid they sound?" I roll my eyes in agreement.

Everyone gets quiet when we enter the classroom with Mr. Johnson standing at the computer, putting up the Proof of the Day. I slide into my seat, smile at Jenn next to me and start working.

I like this teacher, Mr. Johnson. He's probably in his 40's, about my parents' age. He doesn't pretend to be something he's not, like young and cool. I like the precision of geometry. I like drawing the diagrams and solving the formulas in my notebook. I like the way my notebook looks: neatly written and organized with little colored tabs. Geometry is the opposite of my life—it's unmistakable in its certainty, it has clear rules to follow, and there's always one right answer.

"Flye? Can you help me with this? I don't get it at all."

I look at her paper, which is so smudged with erasures that I can barely read it, and then I glance at Mr. Johnson who is occupied with other students. I hand her a clean sheet of paper and we work out the problem together. It's really pretty easy; explaining it to her is the hard part.

"Thanks Flye."

"No problem."

"Oh, uh, Flye? About the stuff in your locker? Uh...I promise you I didn't do it."

I look at her blankly for a second and then realize she wants me to know she's not like the other Belles.

"I know." I smile reflectively and turn back to the board. She does know who did it and she can't tell me.

Stopping by my locker after class, I snatch up my lunch and hurry away to Pandora's Box. I settle myself in the corner and start crunching on an apple as I pick up on two girls in the biology lab.

"—so we should, like, try to be friends with Flye?"

"Well, yeah, I guess so."

I can't tell who this is.

"How 'bout the mall on Saturday?" This from another girl.

"Ugh, I can't. I'm going to the mountains with my family."

"Well, then one day next week after school?"

"Sure, fine, whatever."

Whoa! Someone actually wants to hang out with me? Why?

My thoughts are interrupted by voices from another hole.

"Holy shit Evan. Look what I found."

"That's Jack Daniels, dude. You think Schwartz left it in here?"

"Who else? It's his room."

"So where'd you find it?"

"Behind these books."

"What were you looking for?"

"Nothing, man." I can hear the grin in his voice. "I was just snooping around."

"Yeah, right. You were looking for money."

"Hell no!"

"C'mon, Dusty, what were you looking for?"

"Okay, okay, the damn quiz he's gonna give us. Are ya happy now?"

There's a moment of silence. Evan says, "We gotta tell Brauer, dude. Schwartz could probably get fired for this."

"Seriously? You want to get him fired? Jesus, you're such an Eagle Scout. Who cares if he drinks? You oughta see my old man slam it down. Schwartz likes us. We're gonna get A's in his class."

"So why bother stealing the quiz?"

That stumps Dusty for a minute. I can practically hear him scratching his head. Obviously he's depriving some village of its idiot. We all hear footsteps outside the door.

"Oh, shit! Here he comes. Gimme that, we gotta hide it!"

"Fine, but we have to turn him in…" Evan's whisper fades away as I hear the door opening.

"Dudes! What're y'all doing in here? Looking for me?"

"Yeah, Mr. Schwartz, we've got a question."

Oh, gag a maggot. Dusty's sucking up to him like he's trying to take the chrome off a bumper. I laugh quietly. Then another thought hits me: *Schwartz drinks at school? Maybe that's why he's such an asshole.*

I hear a male voice whispering softly through another vent, too quietly for me to know who it is. "So tomorrow, we're gonna put the other thing in there and then just keep going…"

The voice fades away. *Put what other thing where? Keep going where?*

Chapter Ten

Thank God it's Friday! The locker pranks are getting old. Yesterday, when I opened my locker door, I got slapped in the face by a giant, orange fly swatter. Today, about twenty cans of bug spray roll out. I don't even bother to react; I just pick them up and put them in a bag.

As I'm picking up the cans, Jake comes over and helps me. He doesn't say anything, just puts the cans in the bag, but when we're done and he turns away to leave, I think I hear him mumble, "Sorry."

Then Cody's here, looking antsy and fidgety. "C'mon, Jake, we gotta go."

I watch them go. Halfway down the hall, Jake turns around and gives me a little smile. Okay, so it's not much, but I'll take whatever kindness I can get around here.

When I get to English, Mrs. Meercamp is circulating among the students, collecting the essays that are due today. I've heard kids call her "the Meerkat," and I smile to myself. It fits her: she's little and cute and quick. I glance over at Jake, seeing if I might catch his eye, but he's busy finishing up his essay. Actually, that's good. I wouldn't know what to do if we did make eye contact. I'd just end up feeling like a fool.

The Meerkat reads parts of our essays out loud, carefully avoiding any names or identification. They're about honesty, sports, true love, family, friends, and school spirit. As she continues, I'm more and more anxious. I don't know what I fear the most: that she'll read my essay or that she won't.

"We have time for one more." She starts to read my essay. I focus on not being observed so that I won't give myself away. I don't want anyone to know that this one's mine, but I also want people to know. I want the other kids to say, "Whoa! That's totally awesome, man!" Like that will ever happen. So I doodle on a sheet of paper, sneaking covert looks around the class. Most are listening carefully, while a few are doodling like I am.

She's coming to the end. "In the words of Harvey Fierstein, 'Never be bullied into silence. Never allow yourself to be made a victim. Accept no one's definition of your life; define yourself.'"

The Meerkat is finished. The bell rings and everyone gathers up books and hurries out of the classroom. I walk out, too, but don't get very far. Mrs. Meercamp is right behind me, putting a gentle hand on my shoulder. "Flye, do you have a minute?"

Her voice is what I call "cultured Southern." Her consonants are clear (except for "g" and "r", which are pretty much nonexistent), but her vowels are soft and rounded. "Flye" sounds like "Flah."

"Sure."

Oh no, now what? Am I in trouble for something? Did she find out about Pandora's Box? My heart sinks. That's got to be it.

She sits down at her desk, and I take a seat at a desk in front of her, waiting for her to speak and playing with a pencil to keep me distracted. She picks up a piece of paper off her desk, which I recognize as my essay, and begins to speak.

"Your essay is excellent. Have you heard of Cameo?"

I shake my head. *No. I'm new here. It sounds like an accessories store at a mall.*

"It's our literary magazine that's published once a year. It's very professional. It's student-run and I'm the sponsor. I'd really love to have you join the staff. They're juniors and seniors, but they're bright kids, like you. I think you might make some friends."

"Yeah, maybe. When do you need to know?"

She tells me to take a few days to think it over, and that the magazine doesn't really get started for a week or so.

"Yes, ma'am. Thank you, ma'am." I head out the door.

On the way to my next class, I think about Jake helping me pick up the bug spray and apologizing. For what? That we're both in the same movie called *Nightmare at New Hope High*? I think about being asked to be on the *Cameo* staff and consider it, imagining what it might be like to have older students for friends and to have another safe place to go. Writing for the school magazine could be fun and maybe raise my status here. Of course, it could always just make me more of a target.

I make my way to the Box at lunch time and barely have time to lock the door behind me before I hear, "What the hell do you want, Leah? Stop following me around. God. You're like some kind of stalker."

"Matt, I just miss you. I just want to talk. Don't you miss the way we used to talk all the time?"

"Seriously? All we did was make out—not talk. Besides, you cheated on me."

"I was just trying to make you jealous. And with Evan? He's not even into..." She sighs and I hear her sniffle, like she's trying not to cry. "I just want you back. I'll do anything."

I hear a soft kissing sound and then shuffling as he pushes her away.

"You want to do something for me? Drop dead."

He stomps away, and the door slams. What a douche. I hear soft sobs and almost feel sorry for Leah.

Other voices are coming from the hole closest to my right.

"What the hell, man? What were you doing, picking up all that shit right after the prank?"

I can't tell who it is but the voice is a slithering whisper, filled with a rage so powerful it almost vibrates.

"I just felt sorry for her. I thought I'd help her out."

This sounds like Jake so the other guy must be Cody. They only hang with each other. "Stay away from her. It's just you and me. Like it's always been. Like it's always gonna be."

"Man, I'll always be your friend. But why can't I be friends with her too? She seems nice and—"

"NO!" Cody scream-whispers. "We don't need some little Venus Flytrap hanging around! Besides, I've got a plan, man, and it's gonna make us famous. One through eight, man. That's all we need to know."

Their voices fade, and cold prickles run up and down my spine. They're talking about me. Was that really Cody? It didn't sound like him, all cold and dangerous. But who else could it be? And what the hell is he planning?

Chapter Eleven

I walk in the house and someone grabs me from behind. Before I can turn and punch whoever it is in the gut, I hear, "Hey, lil' sis!"

"Stoney!" He grabs me in a big hug and twirls me around the kitchen, knocking stuff off the counter and toppling over a chair. Mom comes running and swoops up both of us in a family hug. After the obligatory questions ("How was your drive? How's school? Are you getting enough to eat?"), we decide to go to Franklin's Market in Durham, our favorite place for dinner.

When we get home, we try to video-chat with Dad in Guatemala, but the signal is so delayed that it's more frustrating than it's worth. It's always like this when he's away. The three of us have learned to be a family without him. Stoney usually spends more time with Mom and me when Dad's gone. I think he feels more like the man of the house. Mom goes to bed early, and Stoney and I stay up late, talking.

"So now that's Mom's not here, tell me the truth. What's really going on at that school?"

"Oh God, I hate it! The kids are mean. They haze me, and then they ignore me. They can't stop teasing me about my name. I mean, what's the big deal? Just because I don't have some bimbo name like Maddie or Taylor? You saw the bra they put in my locker and then—"

I tell him about the Belles and the Jokes and all the crap they've been doing to me. He listens quietly, his face getting darker and darker with anger. He puts his arm around me and pats my shoulder.

"And Chris is just an asshole, you know? He's hot and he knows it and he's the quarterback and his parents have lots of money and he's the meanest person I've ever met.

"And everyone else seems to have some group to fit into. There's the artsy theater crowd and the music crowd and they all kind of mix together, and the really smart kids are into the Science Club and the Math Club and the Chess Club, and then there's also the druggies and the Goths and the Religious Right and—"

"So you don't really fit anywhere?"

I shake my head and race on. "And then there's this teacher, Mr. Schwartz, except we all call him Gimli 'cause he looks like a dwarf and he sucks up to the Belles and the Jokes and bullies the uncool kids. And I heard that he has a bottle of liquor in his classroom."

I'm aware of tears streaming down my face, and I wipe them away angrily, but not before Stoney sees them. I feel his arm tightening protectively around my shoulders.

He looks at me with incredulous anger. "And this is just the first week? Jesus! I'm going there on Monday, and I'm gonna kick some ass."

"You can't, it's Labor Day."

"Okay fine, I'll go there on Tuesday."

"You can't, you have to get back to school."

"I don't care, okay? I'm going to your school."

I start to smile through my tears. My brother is one of the gentlest people I know. He's thin and wiry and probably couldn't beat anyone up if they had their hands tied behind their back. The thought of him tearing into the school, all Rambo-like, is kind of funny. He sees my smile and knows what I'm thinking. He starts to smile too but then he gets serious.

"What can I do to help you?" He looks at me intently and I know he'll do whatever I say.

"Ask Mom to put me back in middle school."

"Really?"

"Yeah." It sounds more like a question than an answer.

"You sure?"

"No?"

He smiles lopsidedly. "So what do you want me to do?"

"I don't know. I'll be fine, Stoney. I'm getting stronger, and I can take care of myself. I need to learn how to handle this or I'll be running all my life."

I don't mention the Box to him, how it seems like a secret weapon with magic answers. There'll be time for that later.

We sit in companionable silence for a moment. "Were you ever bullied in high school?" I ask.

"I got stuffed in a couple of trash cans, but it's different for guys. You're really young, and you're really smart. And that's hard. Besides, I'm more of an extrovert than you are."

"Do you think someone can be an introvert and also be popular?"

"I don't know. I mean, you can be popular in your own group, but you probably can't be popular in the whole school. You're just you—a really smart, really different kid with underdeveloped social skills."

I lift my clenched fist to punch him in the arm. He draws back, laughing.

"Just kidding. Your social skills will get better as you get older. You're amazing. You're bright. You're observant. And you don't play games. You've always been a really special kid."

He smiles at me sadly. "Do you remember when you were five and I was about twelve? I was starting to go through all that guy stuff about little sisters being a pain in the ass. We were in the living room, and you wanted to play a board game with me."

I nod my head slowly. This isn't a great memory.

"I was so mean to you. I told you to leave me alone and then I ran into my room, but not before I saw tears in your eyes."

"A little while later, you came into my room and I was about to tell you I was sorry. But you just came up to me and gave me a hug and said, "It's okay, Stoney. I just want you to be happy." And then you left and you never asked me to play a board game again.

"What kind of five-year-old would do that? You're amazing, Flye. You're smart, and you're funny, and you're going to be beautiful, as soon as you grow up a little. When you're thirty, you're going to be the hottest rocket scientist on the planet. You already know what you need to do. You just have to keep on doing it."

I hug him and smile, wiping away the last of my tears. "Thanks, Stoney." I pause and grin. "Wanna play a board game?"

We both laugh, and I proceed to beat his ass at Monopoly.

Chapter Twelve

Katie and Taylor are waiting for me by my locker. Oh God, I was hoping that the pranks would be over after the long weekend, that maybe the Belles had just forgotten about me.

"Hey, Flye." Katie is with Taylor, both of them smiling winningly.

I say, "Hey," in a noncommittal sort of way, watching them warily out of the corner of my eye as I gingerly open my locker door. Nothing falls out, and nothing's hanging on the hooks. I sigh in relief and turn back to the girls who are watching me with concern and amusement. "Just checking," I say, with a feeble attempt at a light-hearted laugh.

They laugh, and Katie says, "Do you want to hang with us at the mall after school? Do you have to call your mom or anything?"

I look at her sharply, thinking she's baiting me, but all I see on her open face is a friendly smile.

I actually do have to ask Mom, but I say, "No, yeah, um, I mean, sure, I'll go to the mall with you."

So this is what it feels like, having people asking you to go somewhere. It's nice, but kinda scary; they're so out of my league. It must be Be-Nice-To-An-Outcast Day.

"Great," says Taylor. "Meet you out front after school."

They walk down the hall, butts swaying, hair swinging, and laughing as I watch them, wondering what the hell's going on. A warm hand touches my shoulder as I turn and look into Mr. Lester's kind eyes. "Everything alright, Little Flye Girl?"

"Yeah Mr. Lester, everything's fine."

"No more locker pranks?"

"No sir." I open the door and show him the inside of my locker. "It's all good." I smile as I take out books for English. "Thanks for asking, though."

"If you need anything at all, you just let me know." He smiles, tips his cap and vanishes into the gathering crowd. I wonder briefly if he had anything to do with Katie and Taylor being nice to me. Walking to class, I hear snatches of conversation from the Belles right behind me.

"Awesome party Saturday night, Emily." This is from Leah.

And, of course, Maddie, not willing to be outdone, has to chime in. "Oh, definitely! I just love your pool! And your swim suit was just to die for!"

"First cheerleading practice is today at three. I hear Coach is gonna kick anyone off the team who's late." Jordan's perky little nose is up in the air, floating higher than her sun-streaked pony tail.

"First football game is this Friday." Emily is the ultimate school spirit organizer. Well, after all, she is the head cheerleader. "We've got to think of a really good pep rally. How 'bout *We Will Rock You?* What'd y'all think?"

"Awesome!"

The words flow over and around me as if I'm invisible. This is good. When I was younger, I would have felt lonely and left out. But now, I like being invisible in a crowd. It comes in handy. If I hear anything I really want to know, I'll listen and remember. Otherwise, the noise around me is just that: white noise that defines my space, accompanies me to class, and is immediately silenced when the classroom door closes.

The Meerkat looks at me expectantly when I walk into English, but she doesn't mention *Cameo* at all. I guess she's making good on her promise to give me time to think about it.

I glance over at Jake, but he's got his head on his desk. My eyes meet Cody's instead. I'm surprised, because usually he isn't in here since he goes to special ed instead; mainly, I'm startled because he's looking at me with this cold, reptilian stare, not exactly in a mean way, but unblinking and unfeeling. A shiver runs down my back and I remember the voice in the Box telling Jake to stay away from me.

But his expression only lasts for a second; his face softens and he smiles sweetly. Mrs. Meercamp walks over to him and whispers something in his ear as Cody gathers up his stuff and walks quietly out of the room. I read about Mercutio's and Tybalt's deaths along with the rest of the class, and then I'm on my way to Geometry.

I take my seat next to Jenn. She's still nice to me, especially when she needs help with a problem, which is pretty often, but otherwise she keeps her distance. She's stuck in the middle and we both know it. She's a wannabe, on the outskirts of the Belles, and she probably doesn't want to be there, but she doesn't really know where else to go. So Jenn and I can't have a friendship because she would never be allowed to be friends with me and still keep her status, such as it is, with the Belles.

What we have is more like an arrangement. We sit together in class, we talk when we can get away with it, and I help her with her class work. We do not eat lunch together, walk down the halls together, walk home together, or socialize at all outside of school. When we do see each other out of class, she's with her group and I'm by myself, and we either nod discreetly at each other, or just look the other way. This is just how it is, and it seems to work for both of us. For now, anyway.

The room is quiet. I glance idly around.

"Flye, I don't get number six," Jenn whispers to me.

I glance at Mr. Johnson, who is working with a small group at the white board, and turn back to Jenn. It takes a while for me to explain it to her, but finally, she seems to understand and changes the subject.

"I saw Jake helping you on Friday, you know, with the cans and stuff."

It seems kind of odd that she would just bring up Jake out of nowhere, but I'm curious about him, so I keep the conversation going.

"Yeah, it was really nice of him. So does he, like, just hang out with Cody?"

"Yeah, pretty much. Jake just sort of takes care of him. I mean, Cody's okay, but he just seems so out of it. I've heard he takes a lot of meds." I think of Cody's voice when he was talking to Jake, and how cold and angry it was. I say nothing for a moment, and then I change the subject. This is so weird, having this pretty much normal conversation with a sort-of-popular girl, and I don't really know what to do. So, as usual, I just jump in with both feet.

"Chris really ragged on me in the cafeteria, but he's pretty much ignored me since. Of course, I don't go there anymore. All the drama—it's just not worth it."

Jenn blushes up to her hairline. "The first time? With the bra? That was Emily and them."

She glances around quickly, to make sure no one's overhearing us. "But the other times? Leah and Maddie and them can be mean, but they would never have carried it that far. That was someone else. They're scared they're going to be blamed. They even told Chris not to post the video online. But, you know, he's too cool." She says this with a combination of admiration and disgust.

"Please, please, please, don't tell anyone what I just told you. I'd be in so much trouble. You're so nice to me, and I hate it that you're getting so much shit from people. But I just can't...just promise me..."

I look into her scared face and feel sorry for her. What a place to be in, always worried she's going to do something wrong, always afraid of Emily and the Belles.

I smile at her reassuringly. "I promise I won't ever tell."

Chapter Thirteen

Lunchtime in the Box. I settle myself in the corner with an old comforter I smuggled in, and open my lunch. Yuck! The veggie casserole leftovers from last night's dinner has turned all watery and run all over the nacho chips and salsa. It's gross, but I'm too hungry not to eat it. Even though I've been a vegetarian since the day I was born, I'd love to gulp down a bacon cheeseburger right now.

The voices start filtering in. "How are you Lester? It seems like I never see you anymore."

"Oh, I'm around, I've just been so busy. How was your summer?"

"It was fine; it just went too fast, as always."

"How did it go with the Little Flye Girl?"

I come to attention quickly. *They talk about me? What else have they said that I haven't overheard?*

"Pretty well, I think. She might join *Cameo*. It would be good for her," Mrs. Meercamp continues.

"And how about Jake? How's he doing?"

"It's hard to say," the Meerkat says musingly. "He's so quiet. He always seems tired. He was sleeping in here this morning. He just doesn't put in much effort."

"Let's keep an eye on him. He has it rough at home. His dad makes life hard on him and his mom." Mr. Lester is speaking quietly and I can hear the worry in his voice.

"And how's Cody doing this year?" the Meerkat wants to know. "He came to my class this morning, but I sent him to Sam Dickenson right away. I just can't let him fail English again this year."

Mr. Lester tells the Meerkat about how Cody and Jake promised to follow the Honor Code and to work harder in school this year. "But they're kids. They're gonna make mistakes. I just hope Cody gets it together. And I know you'll help him as much as you can. You know, he seems to be really good at logic games and puzzles, that sort of thing. He was teaching Jake to play 3D chess, and that's not easy."

He's interrupted by a hysterical, unknown voice. "Mr. Lester? Mr. Lester? There's a food fight in the cafeteria."

"It's always something."

I can practically see him tip his cap as he leaves and I hear a crowd roaring in the distance from a hole on my left. I label it "cafeteria."

Other voices focus my attention. They sound like Jake and Cody. "...the city states in... ancient... Greece in...inclu...included Athens, Cor...inth, Argos, Sparta and Troy."

"That's good, Cody, you're doin' better."

"No, I'm not, man. I'm gettin' worse." He sighs. "I'll be sixteen in a couple of months. I'm just gonna drop out. Get a real job. Have my own place. Hey, you could move in with me."

"And leave my mom alone?"

"No, really, man, you could. Plus, it would be safer."

"Safer than what?"

"Than home. You know. I could be away from all of them."

"'Them' who? Your parents? Your parents are nice, man."

"Not my parents, man." Cody's voice drops to a whisper. "You know—the rest of them."

Jake snorts and is interrupted by other voices coming from the hole directly in front of me.

"I can't stop thinking about him. I follow him wherever I can. I dream about him. And I can't tell him. I can't tell anyone." The boy's voice is cracking, like he's ready to cry.

"Jenn, I don't know what to do. I'm gay and I'm not supposed to be. I'll even get kicked out of Boy Scouts. And my parents will kill me. I mean, first me being gay will kill them and then they'll kill me." He sort of laughs and chokes at the same time. It's a sad, desperate sound.

"Evan, it'll be alright. You don't have to tell anyone yet. I mean, you're what, fourteen? How can you even be sure? Things may change for you."

Evan snorts in disbelief. "What do you mean? Like I might wake up one morning and be straight? I've known I was gay since I was five years old. I was obsessed with designing clothes

68

for my sister's dolls. I'm not going to change. And I don't want to. I just want..."

"You just want to be accepted," Jenn finishes his sentence for him.

Again there's silence, broken by the soft sounds of Evan crying. I can imagine Jenn with her arm around him, and I'm glad he has her for a friend.

"Well, he *is* pretty cute. I could have a crush on him too, you know, and then we could compare notes." They both laugh a little.

Other voices catch my attention, coming from the hole to the left of center.

"Chuck, c'mon in. Thanks for taking your lunchtime to talk to me. This won't take long. You're Cody McDaniel's advisor, right?" Mr. Brauer's talking to someone. I quickly label the hole "principal's office."

"Yeah." It's Gimli.

"How's he doing this year?"

"It's hard to say. We've only been in school for a week, so it's hard to say. He doesn't do anything in advisory. He just sits there and draws on his arms and stares off into the distance. There's not much I can do for him if he won't be part of the group."

"Don't you invite some of the students to your room for lunch?"

"Well, yeah, the ones who want to. Cody's never shown any interest."

"Have you invited him?"

"Nope. Don't plan to either."

"Why not?"

"He's a lost cause. I'd rather spend my time on kids who really want to be here."

There's a long pause, and then Mr. Brauer says, "Your attitude sucks, Chuck. You can't be buddies with the popular kids and ignore the ones who really need you."

"I don't know what you're talking about," Schwartz scoffs. "I don't ignore anyone. It's just that kids like Chris and Matt and Danny are into sports and so am I."

Another pause, and Brauer sighs. His voice is soft and thoughtful when he finally speaks again. "Chuck, you and I have known each other since high school."

"Yeah, I know. And I'm grateful to you for giving me this job. After Linda left me, I just fell apart. But I don't think I'm doing anything wrong."

"It's wrong if you exclude some of the kids, and that's what you're doing."

"It is not." Schwartz's voice is rising. I hear him take a deep breath.

"Chuck, remember where we came from? Remember our senior year in high school?"

"I remember."

"We were the nerds, the losers, the ones from the wrong side of town. We were in marching band together. I played trumpet, you played tuba. Remember Greg Jacobson?"

"I remember." Gimli's voice is barely a whisper.

"Remember Homecoming senior year?"

"Yeah, but what's this got to do with anything?"

"It's got everything to do with you. The band was marching at halftime, performing all these tight formations, concentrating on not missing a step, and – "

"I remember all this. Why do you have to bring it up now? It's been twenty years."

Gimli's voice is rising in anger again. This time he doesn't try to calm down. "Someone sneaked into the band room and cut the waistband on my pants. There I was with my pants slipping farther and farther down. And I couldn't do shit with that damned tuba wrapped around me like a python. And I'm in the middle of the field with my pants down around my ankles."

Oh my God, poor Mr. Schwartz! Mr. Brauer continues before I can think another thought.

"And now, here you are, still sucking up to the jocks and dissing the unpopular kids. It's not going to heal anything, you know."

"That's not what I'm doing. I'm fair to all students."

That's not true, and everyone knows it, although now I may understand why you do it. Still, there's got to be something better than trying every day to rewrite your teenage past. Like, isn't that what therapy is for?

"Chuck, I had complaints from parents last year." Brauer tries to continue, but Schwartz cuts him off scathingly.

"I don't know what you're talking about. I've had enough of this shit. I gotta get to my class that you say I don't even know how to teach."

"Chuck, wait—" The door slams as Gimli stomps out.

71

There's a moment of silence, and then Brauer picks up his phone. "Anita, could you please bring Chuck Schwartz's personnel file in here?"

I don't know what to think. I feel sorry for Mr. Schwartz, but that doesn't make it any easier being in his class with him leering and grinning, telling his stupid history jokes and generally making a fool out of himself with the Belles and the Jokes. I think of Jenn and Evan, on the outer fringe, hanging on in fear that one wrong word will get them excommunicated from the sacred circle, and how afraid Evan is to be himself. I think about going to the mall with Taylor and Katie after school today and wonder why they're all of a sudden being so nice to me.

The bell rings. I sigh and head for the door, still lost in my thoughts. When I get to my locker, I gasp in horror and swing around, suddenly remembering: I've left my lunch in the Box.

Chapter Fourteen

Taylor, Katie and I wander through Southside Mall. We're here until 5:30, when Taylor's mom will pick us up and take us home. I feel guilty for just a minute, thinking that I never did get permission from Mom, but then I soothe my conscience by telling myself that I'll be home long before she gets there. She'll never know.

Of course, I've been to the mall before, but only with my parents on forced shopping expeditions. It's different today. The lights are brighter, the background noise is a low rumble of sound with the splashing of a fountain mixed in, and the shops are all brightly lit and beckoning, tempting me inside. The only problem is I just have the twenty dollars that Mom always insists I carry in case of an emergency. This is definitely an emergency.

"Taylor! Let's go to *Pierce Me Please*! Let's get second piercings in our ears."

Taylor turns to me. "Do you want to get a second piercing?"

I blush bright red and want to fall through the floor.

Taylor looks at me quizzically. "Are you okay?"

"Um, yeah. I mean, no, not really. I mean, my ears aren't pierced," I finish in a humiliated whisper.

"Seriously?" Taylor looks at me like I've got three heads but then quickly smiles. "Well, we gotta fix that right now."

"Uh, I don't know. I mean, does it hurt?" Now I'm embarrassing myself; I sound like such a wuss.

She looks at me like I'm about five. "Yeah, you'll probably pass out from the pain."

She sees the look of pure panic on my face and laughs. "Of course not, silly. You won't even feel it. They even put hypoallergenic earrings in so you won't get an infection. 'Cause if you get an infection, it'll go straight to your brain and you'll die."

Again my face gives me away and she doubles over in laughter. "God, you're gullible. Let's go. Katie's probably already done."

I follow reluctantly, wishing I were home but not wanting to disappoint them. For all her razzing me, I'm starting to like Taylor a lot.

After we're all finished, we head for *Phantasmagoria*, the coolest accessories store ever (according to Katie). I keep pushing back my hair so everyone can see my new fake diamond studs. We make a beeline to the earring counter

"Look at these, Flye," Katie is holding up a pair of dangling amethyst earrings that would hang down to my shoulders. "Here, hold them up, see how they look."

I hold the earrings up to my ears. They're really pretty, but glancing at the tag I see that they're twenty-five dollars. "Yeah, they're nice, but I'm gonna look some more."

"Here, Flye, try these." Taylor holds up more earrings. For the next few minutes, they find pair after pair of earrings for me to try that I can't afford; my ears are sore and I'm starting to panic.

What am I going to do? Why did I ever agree to come on this shopping trip from Hell in the first place? What was I thinking?

"Yo, Flye." I see that Katie's holding up yet another pair and I'm ready to tell them I don't have much money left when I see that these earrings have been marked down to five dollars.

I'm so relieved, I yelp, "Oh yeah! That's what I'm talkin' 'bout!" I buy them on the spot.

We all high five and walk to the food court. I never realized how famished shopping could make me. We get fries and chocolate shakes. We're sitting at a table in the middle of the enormous room when Katie yells out, "Chris! Matt! Hey guys!"

Oh. My. God. Is she insane? Now Taylor is joining her, jumping up and down and waving maniacally, and here come Chris and Matt. I think about going to the bathroom to hide— seeing them has made me feel like I really do have to puke—but it's too late.

"Hey Katie, hey Taylor." Chris looks at me with an arrogant smirk dripping with insolence and drawls, "Hey, Flye."

I mumble, "Hey," and keep my eyes on my shake even though I have absolutely no appetite now.

"So, you girls going to the game this Friday?" Chris is talking to Katie and Taylor and completely ignoring me.

"Well, duh. Of course," they giggle, twirling their matching pony tails and rolling their eyes. Then Katie turns to me and says, "Wanna come, Flye?"

My mouth drops open so far you could drive a car through it, but I recover quickly. "Uh, yeah, sure. Uh, unless I have something else to do."

Chris looks me up and down scornfully, his thoughts clearly readable on his face. *Like what? Baking cookies with your mamma?*

Taylor gives him the evil eye and he backs off. *Whoa! What a ballsy move! I wish I knew how to do that.*

Chris and Matt start to leave. "See ya, ladies and Flye." He and Matt laugh as they walk away.

Taylor turns to me. "You've just got to ignore Chris. He's moody. But he's a nice guy when you get to know him."

Nice? Compared to whom? Adolf Hitler?

"And Ohmygod," Katie gushes. "Those eyes! That hair! I saw him without his shirt at football practice. I would do anything for that boy," she leers at both of us, rolling her eyes and licking her lips lasciviously, "and I do mean anything."

Taylor is laughing so hard she's practically falling off her chair, tears rolling down her face. I try to laugh too, but it feels awkward. I mean, this is the guy who goes out of his way to humiliate me. The thought of touching him grosses me out.

"Yeah, really?" Taylor is leading her on. "Like what? Third base?"

"Oh, honey, forget the bases! It'd be a homerun all the way, girl!"

I guess I know what a homerun is, but what are the bases? I think first base is kissing but the rest—I have no idea. I certainly don't have any personal experience, and it's not the kind of thing I'd ask my mom.

They fall over laughing, and Taylor gasps, "Well, girlfriend, you're gonna have to get in line, 'cause he's crushin' on Emily."

"Really?" Her lips tremble and her eyes well up.

Taylor stops in mid-sentence, looking horrified. "Oh, no! I'm *sorry*! I didn't know you were really into him. I would never have said that. Besides, I heard Leah tell Maddie that all he wants is for them to be the power couple. I don't think he's really all that into her." She smiles and gives Katie a hug. "There's still hope."

Katie perks up a little and wipes her eyes as Taylor glances at her watch. "Oh shit! It's almost 5:30. My mom will kill me if we're late!"

We run through the mall like escapees from a psych ward, narrowly missing baby strollers and an old woman leaning on a cane, but we make it to the main entrance just as Taylor's mom pulls up in her SUV. Panting, we pile in the car and pull away as if we're off to a fire.

"Did you girls have fun? Yes?" She answers her own question. "Taylor, I've got another house to show right away. As soon as you get home, you need to get started on homework. No computer time 'til everything is finished, y'hear?"

Taylor mumbles something incoherent, which I guess means, "Yes, Ma'am," and turns bright red. A surge of sympathy flows through me. I mean, it's not like my parents are cool or anything, but they'd never embarrass me in front of my friends like that.

When I get home, I take a few things out of the fridge so that it'll look like I'm in the middle of fixing dinner when Mom gets home and go into my room, flopping on the bed. I take out the ridiculous, dangly, peace-sign earrings and start to laugh. I went to a mall. With two semi-popular girls. Holy crap.

Chapter Fifteen

I'm at my locker, getting lunch stuff out. Katie and Taylor breeze by on the way to the cafeteria, calling over their shoulders, "C'mon, Flye! Sit with us." They don't stop, and I see them plunk down at a table next to the Belles and the Jokes. Way too close to the enemy for me. I don't have a chance to make up a lie, so I just walk quietly down to the Box, looking around for any color changes from the Great Unknown. There are none, and a twinge of disappointment tweaks at me. I secretly want this room to be some kind of space-time portal and Mr. Lester to be really magical, but the truth has got to be that I'm making it all up because I'm so desperate to find a way to fit in here.

As I look around the Box, my stomach lurches and my breath stops. The remains of yesterday's lunch have all been cleared away and my comforter is neatly folded in the corner with my lunch box. Nothing is the way I left it. Before I can have a full-blown panic attack, however, I hear voices coming from a hole on my right.

"So how did it go yesterday?" It's Maddie.

"Oh, you know, fine. We just hung out at the mall, got earrings, saw Chris and Matt." It's Katie. I'm grateful that she doesn't mention the fact that I didn't have pierced ears. That would be all over school like white on rice.

"Matt went to the mall without telling me?" Maddie's voice rises to a cat-like screech.

"Maddie, you gotta give him some space or you're gonna lose him. Guys don't like to be smothered."

"Oh, really, Miss Ho? And how many boyfriends have you had?"

"Well, yeah, but I have brothers..." Katie trails off with no other defense.

Maddie changes the subject. "So how did it go with Flye?"

"You know, she's actually pretty fun. It was kinda like taking a little sister shopping, wasn't it, Katie?"

"Yeah, she's pretty cool."

"And she's going to the game with us this Friday,"

"Bringing her to the game is a great idea. That's just brilliant." Maddie's all over it. "And then afterwards..."

First they bully me and now they wanna be friends? I guess I played their game right and acted cool enough for them to respect me. Maybe now they think I'm okay to be in their group.

Another voice from the left distracts me. It's a soft whisper with sibilant "s's," low and threatening. "You know it's time to get started, so what are you waiting for?"

I can't tell who it is, but I recognize Cody's voice answering, "Yeah, I know man, but I don't want to. What if I get caught? My parents will be so mad, and I hate it when they're mad." His voice sounds soft and young, like a little kid whining that he doesn't want to go to bed.

"Oh, what's the matter wif widdle Cody?" The voice hisses snakelike through the tunnel of the vent and into my ear, and I recoil in horror and recognition. This is Cody, too. It's Cody's voice, cold and harsh, full of malice. I freeze on the spot, holding my breath, my flight instinct dialed up as high as it goes.

"Is widdle Cody scared?" The whisper rises on a wind of fury. "Well, get over it!" The whisper is a scream and Cody whimpers piteously.

I think seriously about finding Mr. Lester to go help him when I hear, "We're helping that fuckin' bitch Levinson troubleshoot the school computers. We've got the password. Get off your ass, man. It's time to have some fun." He laughs maniacally, the sound raising the hairs on my arms and the back of my neck.

"Everything alright in here, Cody?" I hear the door open and Mr. Lester's quiet voice interrupts. "I thought I heard you talking to someone."

"Oh, no, I'm fine, just doing some homework." Cody's voice is soft and friendly and I'm sure he has that little half-smile on his pasty face, his colorless eyes focused on the floor.

Mr. Lester pauses for a moment. "Well, good, I'm glad to hear it. It seems like you're working hard and I'm proud of you. You have a good afternoon." I hear the door close behind him.

"Let's go," Cody says in the harsh whisper.

The door opens and closes again, and the room is silent behind him. I lean against the wall for support, cold sweat soaking my hair, and fold my shaking hands around my knees drawn up to my chest. This can't be real. How can Mr. Lester, who seems to be everywhere and know everything, not know about Cody and this...this other Cody? How can he buy that homework-doing, trying-harder crap? I guess he's not as magical as I wanted him to be. And Cody...I hear that snake-like whisper in my head and start to shake again. Cody is sicker than I ever thought. He's sicker than anyone in this school knows.

Chapter Sixteen

When I get home, Mom's already there, saying, "Oh, Flye, remember my book club friends are coming over tonight?"

No, I don't remember. I can't keep track of the details of my life and now I'm supposed to remember hers? I smile my poodle smile at her, where I bare my teeth and look happy, and she thinks everything's peachy keen with me.

"Sure, Mom. Fine. Have fun," I say. Book club nights usually are a potluck dinner that turns into a lot of female bonding and wine drinking, which then turns into a really late night.

She follows me into my room, which is a mess, as usual. "Yard sale eclectic," I call it, except you really can't see the carpet for all the clothes, books, stuffed animals and a couple of moldy cookies. She looks around in disgust, says something about cleaning up this mess before she just turns a hose on it, and closes the door.

She's right. My room is a mess. I kick everything under my bed, including the cookies—they might come in handy someday if I ever need a dose of penicillin—and pull my orange and green comforter up over the bed. There. All done.

I flop on the bed, crank up Joni Mitchell's *The Circle Game* and check out my wall online. Nothing new there, so I start chatting with Rebekkah.

Loneshewolf:	hey, girl, whaddup
Bekkahsavatar:	not much, whaddup with you
Loneshewolf:	a lot, really
Bekkahsavatar:	yeah? Like what? r u ok?
Loneshewolf:	yeah, I'm fine just a lot happening at school. I hate it
Bekkahsavatar:	oh I know u do but just hang in there things will get better it hasn't even been two weeks yet
Loneshewolf:	yeah I know but it's more than that
Bekkahsavatar:	what's wrong?
Loneshewolf:	omg how much time do u have
Bekkahsavatar:	all night WHAT'S WRONG!?
Loneshewolf:	I'm kinda in a mess
Bekkahsavatar:	OMG!!!! WHAT HAVE YOU DONE NOW??????

Loneshewolf: ok I'll tell u if you'll just listen. and stop SCREAMING at me!!!

Bekkahsavatar: ok, sorry, I'm listening

I tell her about all the hazing and how I found the Box and how I've been going there every day. I tell her about all the conversations I've heard and what I know about people at school. She doesn't reply much, just an occasional "OMG" or "then what?"

I tell her about Gimli being a former geek and how he makes other geeks' lives hell. I tell her about Jenn not being able to be my friend but Katie and Taylor wanting to hang with me which seems bizarre but nice and then I tell her about what I heard Cody do today and how he's like two different people.

Bekkahsavatar: R U CRAZY???? U hafta tell someone. he could be doing anything you're just scared

Well yeah, that's true; I am scared of Cody, but not as much as I'm scared of losing the Box and not knowing everything that's going on. Even more than that, I'm scared of being caught. Because if I think life at NHH is hard now, the shit will really hit the fan then.

Loneshewolf: well, I think someone already knows about the box

| Bekkahsavatar: | WHAT????!!!!! U R SERIOUSLY INSANE WHAT DO U MEAN SOMEONE KNOWS????? |

I tell her about how mysterious Mr. Lester can be, how he just appears out of nowhere and how the door was left open in the first place, like someone had invited me in, and about how he's always around when I leave the Box. I don't tell her about the hallucination I had. She already thinks I'm a nut job, so why make it any worse?

| Bekkahsavatar: | all I can tell u is to not go there anymore. really, for someone who's supposed to be so smart, you are doing a really dumb thing. DON'T GO THERE AND TELL SOMEONE ABOUT IT!!!!!!! AND YOU HAVE TO TELL SOMEONE ABOUT CODY!!!!!!!!!!!!!!! |

I can tell she's getting pissed, and I hate it when Bekkah is mad at me.

| Loneshewolf: | alright, I won't go there anymore and I'll tell someone about Cody. Happy now? |

Bekkahsavatar:	yeah, but you gotta promise me
Loneshewolf:	i promise
Bekkahsavatar:	really? on your honor?
Loneshewolf:	yeah, really. on my honor.

One of the best things about chatting online is that she can't see me crossing my fingers when I promise her.

We chat for a couple of hours, and then Bekkah's mom tells her that she needs to get some sleep because it's a school night. It's almost midnight and the women downstairs are still partying, so I fall into bed and plug in my ear buds, but I can't stop the incessant chatter in my head.

Questions swirl through my mind: *Should I tell someone about Cody?*

Really, what's there to tell? I can't prove that it was him I heard.

Yes, you can. You heard Mr. Lester talking to him, but if you tell him, he'll know about the Box.

Yeah but I think he already knows, so maybe I should just tell him.

Yeah but then you'll have to stop going to the Box and you ABSOLUTELY CANNOT give that up!

But maybe I should stop going to the Box.

See answer above. You're not doing anything wrong. Just practice ostrich philosophy and keep your head in the sand. You're just an innocent bystander; just a little fly on the wall.

I argue with myself until I finally fall asleep.

Chapter Seventeen

Mrs. Meercamp turns on the projector for the Smart Board, but I've got my head in my hands and my eyes are drooping. Gasps erupt all around me and someone from the Jokes' side of the room mumbles, "What the hell," as I jerk awake and am fixated by the screen, which is flashing like lightning strikes against the words "Die Fascist Pigs," written in what looks like dripping blood. Even Mrs. Meercamp is transfixed for a few seconds before she flips off the projector and, hearing commotion from other rooms around us and teachers gathering in the hall, walks to the doorway.

"Class! I just need a moment. I want everyone to open their books and start reading quietly." Yeah, right, like that's going to happen.

"What's a fascist?" Emily asks. She pronounces it "fassist."

Chris replies, "The first one across the finish line, sweetness."

"What does it mean? Are we gonna die?" Someone else sounds panicky.

"No, it's just a prank, not a death threat. Get a grip," a kid in a computer logo t-shirt says scornfully.

"Maybe it's part of a vegan protest, talking about pigs."

I hear some sighs from my side of the room and am momentarily grateful that there are still some reasonably intelligent people in this school.

"Someone must have hacked the server if other rooms are getting the same message."

"Who's good enough with computers to have done this?"

"Anyone could have done it; all they needed was the password to the server."

I can practically feel my blood freezing. I remember Cody's harsh, cold voice from yesterday, and I can see his pale, reptilian eyes as I hear the words in my head: *"We have the password, it's time to have some fun..."*

I steal a glance at Jake but he's just gazing out the window, looking completely detached and I wonder how much he knows about Cody's other side. I have to tell someone. I'll tell Mr. Lester at lunch today.

Not so fast. You really don't have any proof yet. But what if you could get some? Then you could really do some good and not just run around with mindless conjectures like everyone else.

Mrs. Meercamp is back in the room before I can make up my mind. "Alright, listen up, everyone."

The noise subsides, and the room comes to attention as she explains, "Evidently someone has been tampering with the school's computer system and put this message on every classroom's screen."

The class starts to murmur again and she quiets them. "This is just a prank. There's nothing to be afraid of. Mrs. Levinson is working on it and the security team is scouring the building."

Someone asks, "Is this a bomb threat?"

"Let's not get carried away." She goes on to talk about how rumors get started and how we should not get into trauma-drama mode and what fascism means.

Finally she says, "Mr. Brauer has instructed all of us to continue with our day as usual. We will have a writing lab so please check out a laptop. Then start writing your impressions of *Romeo and Juliet*."

Quiet whispering continues throughout the room, and I hear several people start to call the message the "Pig Virus." I get a laptop, frantically trying to remember what I learned about coding from Steven. All I need is a password.

I remember being in the Box and hearing Cody telling Jake that they were going to be famous and to remember "one through eight." Glancing around furtively, I log in under administrator and type one, two, three, four, five, six, seven, eight, hold my breath and hit enter.

I'm in. I laugh to myself, thinking that if the password is that obvious, they deserve to get hacked. I can't believe it hasn't happened sooner.

I access the school's C drive, find the Pig Virus, open it, read the code, and find the IP address: 192.168.31.6. Now all I have to do is find out who it belongs to.

Class is winding down. I log out, clear all cookies, run the program cleaner and walk toward the computer cart.

"Mrs. Meercamp?" I put on my most innocent and sincere face. "May I check out this computer over lunchtime? I'm really on a roll right now and I'd hate to lose it."

"Of course, Flye. Just go ahead and take it now."

I must look surprised because she says, "Oh, it's alright. I trust you, and I know which laptop you've got." She winks at me, smiles, and says, "Happy writing!"

At lunch, I'm in the Box. I log on to my personal email account and send a brief message to Steven.

Hey, Steven, I need your help. If I give you an IP address can you tell me who it's from? Thanks, Flye.

P.S.: Also, if you could get the login and password that would be great. I owe you, dude.

It's been a couple of months since I've talked to him, but I'm sure he'll come through for me. He loves doing this stuff, and he goes to a high school that specializes in technology, so he eats, breathes, and sleeps it.

Voices from my left distract me. "I bet it was Trevor. He's always messing around with computers and shit." This sounds like Danny.

"No, he's too squeaky clean. I bet it was that dude from last year who got kicked out for putting a virus on all the school's computers." It's Matt.

"I don't know who you're talkin' about, man. We weren't even here last year."

"Well, duh, I know that. My sister told me about him. He ended up going to juvie for a while. Yeah, man, I bet it was him."

Someone else laughs. "Yeah right. Like he came back from juvie just to hack our computers? Again?"

There are a few more chuckles, and I'm glad that they're giving Matt crap about such a stupid comment.

The laptop bleeps, and there's an email from Steven: "IP address belongs to Cody McDaniel. Login: RebDoomerII. Password: @1U$ib**!"

Chapter Eighteen

Some of the kids try to talk about the Pig Virus in Ancient History, but Gimli just blows it off, saying it's not that big of a deal. Then he announces a pop quiz and the room is quiet for the rest of the period. The silence is broken only by the clack of the keys on Schwartz's laptop. He's probably emailing or chatting with someone; I'm sure that's not a lesson plan he's working on, and I'm also sure we'll never get this quiz back. He's famous for giving out pop quizzes and then dumping them in the trash afterwards. It's just his way to get us to shut up and leave him alone.

I find myself obsessing about the email I got from Steven and I know I'm going to drive myself crazy until I get home and can hack into Cody's computer. All I can see are the words: "IP belongs to Cody McDaniel." I just know I'm going to blurt it out if I don't take my mind off it. I focus on the quiz, but finish it in about ten minutes.

I need another distraction, so I pull my hair down in front of my face and watch Jake. He has his backpack propped on his lap and I can see him texting. His black hair curls around his shoulders and down the back of his t-shirt, and his long fingers fly across the keypad as he types, then smiles, and then types some more.

The bell rings. I turn in my quiz and leave.

Sitting at my lab table in biology, I start thinking again about Cody. There's only forty-five more minutes 'til I get home. I imagine what I'll find on his computer besides the Pig Virus message: he's hacked into the school records and changed his grades, he's changed Jake's grades, he's gone to disgusting porn sites.

Mrs. Klitchner is announcing a new assignment, and I return to the present in the middle of her speech. We need to start bringing our cell phones to class, starting tomorrow, because we're going to use them to text answers during discussions into her projector. We can all read what everyone texts and continue the discussion via cell phone. How cool! There's just one problem—my cell phone is an ancient flip phone without even a texting keyboard. I'll have to buy a new phone if I want to get any comments typed in before the next ice age.

The rest of the class is excited, too, about switching up the routine. It's not like we'll say anything different in our text messages than we would out loud, but this is just a much cooler way to have a class discussion.

After school, Katie and Taylor stop me by my locker. "Hey, Flye," says Taylor, "wanna go get ice cream?"

God, no! I'm jumping out of my skin, practically salivating to get to Cody's computer.

"Oh, I can't," I say, faking disappointment. "I have to go home right away and fix dinner. My mom will kill me if I don't."

They roll their eyes in sympathy and Katie says, "Well, see ya tomorrow."

"'K," I call after them. They bounce away, already on a mission to somewhere else.

I sprint home, and I'm in my room, opening my laptop in a wild frenzy and downloading the coding program Steven sent me. I open the program, sign in with Cody's login and password, and I'm in. Holy shit! I'm looking at Cody's desktop. His background is some ninja warrior Manga-looking graphics, and his files are all arranged neatly. I was expecting to find links to death and destruction sites. This all looks pretty innocent. I don't see anything vaguely representing the Pig Virus. He must have deleted it, because it had to have been here.

I look at his browsing history and there's nothing remarkable there either, just a bunch of emails with Jake about what time to get online and play games. Then I go to his bookmarks. There's nothing there but a lot of links to gaming sites. I can't believe this; there's absolutely nothing incriminating here.

His screen saver starts and I watch in frozen amazement as words written in what looks like red, dripping blood, just like the pig message, appear: "FOUR TWENTY FOREVER."

What the hell does that mean?

I search "four twenty" on my computer and get thousands of hits on smoking marijuana. *Cody's a pothead?*

Chapter Nineteen

I'm in the Box, playing with my new smartphone. I begged, pleaded and whined for one last night until Mom finally broke down and bought it for me. After I told her I needed it for a school assignment, she caved.

I log into Cody's laptop and check his browsing history. There's still nothing incriminating there but before I can snoop any further, I'm interrupted.

"—so here's the plan, man." Voices are coming from my right and I sit up straighter, coming to attention. It's Cody, and I wait tensely to hear if he's talking to himself again.

"You're going to join Science Club—"

"What?" Jake cuts him off and I breathe a sigh of relief. At least Cody's talking to another human being. "What for? I don't have time for that shit, and besides, I hate science."

"Just listen to me and do what I say." Cody's voice is verging on the crazy side. "You're gonna join Science Club, and your project is gonna be the effects of fertilizer on garden plants."

"What the hell? That's the craziest shit I've ever heard." Jake is flabbergasted but Cody cuts him off.

"Don't ever call me crazy, you fuckin' idiot." It's Crazy Cody's voice, raspy, cold and deadly. Chills run down my spine and I wish I had a spy hole in here so I could see the look on Jake's face. "You're missing the point, as always." Cody laughs, a high-pitched, manic sound.

"Okay, fine, just calm down. Tell me the plan," Jake says soothingly. Apparently he's been through this with Cody before, as I hear Cody take a deep breath and proceed in his normal voice.

"The point is the fertilizer."

Other voices interrupt them from the center and I hear my name.

"So Flye is going to the game with us." It's Katie.

"Great," says Maddie. "We'll all sit together and then I'll ask her over to my house. My parents are going out of town. My brother is going to—"

"—but I don't get it. What's the big deal with fertilizer?"

"—that'll be totally awesome!"

"Just trust me, man. I know what I'm doing. Remember how I said I was gonna make us famous—?"

I'm getting dizzy listening to two conversations at the same time, not knowing what anyone's talking about. On the one hand, Cody is manipulating Jake into doing something crazy, and if I overhear their plan, I'll be the only one who knows about it. On the other hand, Maddie and Taylor are talking about me? They're going to invite me somewhere? This is freakazoid.

The bell rings, everyone stops talking, doors slam shut, and it's quiet in the Box. I stay still for a minute, trying to process everything I've just heard. Maddie's having a party at her house after the game and I'm invited? And Cody wants Jake to join the Science Club and grow plants? That just seems so random. And why would the Belles personally invite me to one of their parties?

Chapter Twenty

I sit at my lab table in biology and take out my new phone. Leah walks by and says, "Well, well, well. Look who got a brand new smart phone. Lemme see." She goes to pick it up without waiting for my answer.

I grab the phone before she can and move it to the other side of my table.

She looks as if I just slapped her. (Not a bad idea, but luckily for her, I don't believe in violence.)

"Bitch," she says, just loud enough for most of the class to hear as she moves on back to her table. She whispers to Maddie, their hands in front of their mouths, both staring at me. Then they both burst out laughing.

"Shut up, Leah!" It's Jake, from across the room. I couldn't be more shocked if he bent down on one knee and proposed to me.

"Oh, I'm so sorry, Jake. I didn't know she was your girlfriend. Are you two a couple now? I'm so glad! I've been sooooo worried about who will be Homecoming king and queen. Looks like that's settled."

There's more laughter from the back table, but it ends immediately when Mrs. Klitchner walks into the room.

We get right down to work as usual, but the discussion is really fun using our phones. It's amazing what a little novelty can do for something as boring as cell structure.

The bell is going to ring in about a minute. I start putting my books away and, as I do, my phone vibrates in my hand. A new text message reads, "You're ugly and stupid. No one likes you here. No one wants you here. Why don't you just die!?" The number is blocked.

I glance around the room, trying not to be noticed. Everyone's in some stage of packing up; I don't see anyone who looks suspicious.

Walking to my locker, I see Jake over in a corner, talking to Cody. I gaze at Jake for just a second, wondering why he stood up for me. I guess he can sense me looking at him because he glances up, sees me, and gives me a quick smile.

We continue to stare at each other, both of us smiling a little. My stomach is fluttering, but not in a bad way, and I can feel my face warm from my neck to my hairline. Jake is blushing faintly too, and he glances away awkwardly. I look away too—at my shoes. Which is totally stupid, like what a five-year-old would do. When I look back up, he's still looking at me and we're both even redder.

Shit.

I gather up my stuff and walk out the door as nonchalantly as possible, as if I hadn't just proved my total lack of social skills. I cringe just thinking about it.

My phone beeps and it's another text message. "You are scum. You are lower than scum. I hate you, you pathetic sack of shit." The number is blocked again. Great. This is now officially the worst day of my life. I shove my phone back into my bag, but a lump stays lodged in my stomach and chest.

I walk out the front door along the sidewalk and hear a car roaring by. Something heavy whizzes past my left ear. Turning, I see a full soda can heading toward the lake. The car is too far away by now to get a good look, but it's a red convertible with two boys in front and two girls in back. One of the girls has long, black hair.

I collapse in the grass, shaking with fear and adrenaline. If that soda can had been half an inch closer, it would have hit me in the head. I could have been really hurt. Suddenly, I'm not scared anymore. I'm just really pissed off. Who do those people think they are? They think they can get away with anything they want just because they're hot and rich and drive cool cars and radiate an aura of intimidation and glamour.

I turn around and walk back to school, determined to tell someone everything that's been going on, and I see Mr. Lester standing out front, holding an unopened soda can. What the...? Is that the same can they just threw? If it is, that means it would've had to have made a ninety-degree turn in mid-air to go from where their car was to Mr. Lester's hand.

I stare at him with my mouth open, shaking my head. He walks toward me, popping the can open and taking a long swallow. "Are you alright, Little Flye Girl?" His eyes search mine with deep concern and suddenly all my anger and courage drain away, and all I want to do is cry.

My eyes well up, my throat clinches, and I don't trust myself to speak. He keeps looking at me and then hands me a cold bottle of water which I drain in about two gulps.

"Better now?" He smiles at me kindly, but his eyes are still worried.

I nod, finally able to speak and say, "Yeah, I'm okay."

"Do you know who those kids were?"

Well, yeah, one of them was Leah, but I can't prove it since they were too far away.

"No," I say. He nods thoughtfully and then says, "You don't have to do everything alone, you know. It's okay to ask for help."

I look at him for a long time, wondering if that's true, and then say, "Mr. Lester, if I rat people out, it'll only make everything worse for me." *And I'll lose the Box.*

"Sometimes you have to lose something in order to get something that's even better." He stares at me thoughtfully, and I have a strange feeling that he can read my mind.

"Really, Mr. Lester, I'm okay."

"Uh huh." He looks at me with blatant disbelief. "So what happened today?"

I tell him about Biology, about Leah trying to take my phone, and then her and Maddie laughing at me. I tell him about Jake standing up for me and then how the girls started ragging on both of us. I don't tell him about the hate texts or about Jake and me having a moment at the lockers.

"Jake stood up for you?" He's pleased and surprised.

"Yeah, I guess so." I don't know what else to say, so I stand up and start picking up my stuff.

"Not so fast there. I want you to do something for me."

"Now what? I just want to go home." It comes out as a whine.

"Just come with me, please."

I start to follow him down the hall. "Where are we going?" I ask, as we turn into the freshman hall and then stop outside a door. Oh man, it's the Meerkat's room. He's gonna make me tell her.

Chapter Twenty-One

"Mr. Lester," I begin, but he cuts me off.

"Shhh. Just let me handle this."

The Meerkat comes to the door. "Why Lester, how nice to see you! Hello, Flye. What are you two doing here?"

"Well, I just walked Flye down here. Maybe she can help y'all out some."

Turning back to me, he says, "Little Flye Girl, I'll leave you here to get acquainted."

"Thank you, Mr. Lester." I try to smile, but it doesn't work. *Get acquainted with whom? The Meerkat? I already know her.*

Mrs. Meercamp smiles at me and says, "How lucky you're here. We're one girl short."

I must look like a blank sheet of paper because she says, "Oh, I'm sorry. I should explain. This is *Cameo*. This is our first meeting. We're working on the format. The publishing program we use is complicated, and Toni, our expert, is absent, so we're all just muddling through. Do you think you could help us out, since you're so good with computers and all?"

"Sure." I mean, not really, but what else am I supposed to say?

"That's excellent."

I glance around the room. The kids in this club look different than the Belles. Older. Friendlier. Not so caught up with appearances.

The Meerkat motions to a tall, slender girl in an Indian-print skirt that swishes the floor as she walks. Her feet are bare, and I see a butterfly tattoo on her left ankle. From across the room, she looks really tan, but as she gets closer, I can see that she's covered with millions of freckles. Her hair is bound up in a purple bandanna, but I'm guessing she's got red hair under there. Who else would freckle like that?

She smiles at me, holds out her hand, and says, "Hey. My name's Lily. Who are you?"

"I'm Flye," I stammer a little. She's so self-possessed— friendly, but I can just tell that no one gives her any crap. "It's nice to meet you."

"Flye?" She turns around to the other kids and I brace myself. Oh, no, not again. "Did y'all hear that? She's so fly, it's her name." She turns back to me and says, "We've heard about you. Good to have you here. The Meerkat said you might join us."

I'm astonished into silence. I didn't know anyone called Mrs. Meercamp by her nickname to her face. I glance at her out of the corner of my eye, but she's just laughing and smiling along with the rest of them.

"C'mon over." Lily motions to me. "Meet everyone else."

There are about ten girls and a couple of guys. Camille is blond, tiny, and shy, and Georgia is short, round, and has skin the color of coffee with caramel cream. She has two dimples in her baby face, and it seems like she laughs more than anything else. I like her immediately.

Jerrod is tall and skinny with curly, red hair, and a hoop in his left ear, and Dexter is very large, with shoulder length curly, brown hair, and wire-rim glasses. We sit down around a long table.

I wait to see who's going to talk first. Dexter jumps right in. "The Meerkat showed us your essay. Girl, you can write!"

I blush and smile, and Lily says, "Yeah, we love your writing. We don't just put the magazine together—we're all writers, too. We've won awards for the last three years."

"Yeah, for as long as you've been here, Lily." Georgia laughs. "What are we gonna do next year when you're gone?"

"Next year is a long time away," Lily says. "Anything can happen." She directs her full attention to me and says, "Do you have any questions? Do you accept bribes?" Everyone laughs, and Lily goes on, "Because we really need you."

"Um, bribes maybe," I laugh. "I wrote for my middle school's newspaper last year, so I'm pretty familiar with it all."

"Cool!" Dexter exudes enthusiasm. "All y'all, listen up! She's in!"

"Cool!" Camille is smiling widely, but Lily notices the hesitation on my face and says, "I hope so. Just keep thinking about it."

They all start talking about the new magazine's format, and Georgia shares some of her graphic designs, which are the best I've ever seen. I'm feeling a little cautious since they all know each other so well and are so relaxed together. I'm content just listening to them, but that doesn't last for long.

"Flye, do you know any publishing programs?" Georgia wants to know.

"Yeah, actually I know several." We all move over to the computers, I pull up a program and start with a very basic format.

"Now that's what I'm talking about," Dexter yells, and several of us, including me, laugh. He's just so out there, you can't not like him.

We finally have a pretty snazzy cover when the Meerkat says, "Alright, y'all, it's five o'clock. Time to go."

Some of us groan, including me. Oh no! I was having such a good time!

"So, what do you think, Flye? Are you in?" Lily asks.

"Absolutely." I nod enthusiastically, just so they understand that I'm really glad to be a part of this group.

Georgia gives me a hug and says, "That's great, girl!"

"Oh, and Flye?" Lily stops me again. "Do you want to have lunch with us at school next Friday?"

I don't say anything because I don't understand. Freshman and sophomores have lunch at a different time than juniors and seniors. Finally I say, "Sure, but I don't know how to manage that."

Georgia says, "We have a special lunch arrangement on Fridays. We get a double lunchtime and we eat in the Meerkat's room. Supposedly, we work on the magazine."

Someone yells, "Oh, c'mon, Georgia, we work. Sometimes."

"We mostly talk about whatever interests us. And we do work. But we also just hang out. So whaddaya think? Wanna have lunch with us?"

I think for just a second about missing the Box, but I blow it off. It's just one day a week, right? What difference can that make?

"Absolutely."

I walk home, the lyrics to *I Can See Clearly Now* running through my head.

Chapter Twenty-Two

It's the day of the first game, and before I know it, Katie and Taylor are waiting for me after school at the snack stand, getting a soda and a bag of what looks like lumpy snot.

"Hey, Flye," they cry in unison and Katie gives me a little half-hug. *Seriously? Like now we're besties?*

"Want some boiled peanuts?" asks Taylor, holding up the lumpy snot bag.

"Uh, no thanks, I'll just get some popcorn." Once I have a greasy paper bag full of buttery popcorn, I wait for them to take the lead. I've never been at a football game, and I have no idea what to do.

"Let's go walk around the field and watch the guys warm up," says Katie.

"All the guys or just one?" Taylor teases her.

"Oh, Taylor, it's not my fault you can't even imagine dating the quarterback, bless your heart." She smiles sweetly, dimpling her cheeks. This is standard procedure in the South. You can insult someone all you want as long as you add "bless your heart." One should never be rude.

"Puh-lease, as if you could ever date Chris. Your teeth still stick out so far you could eat an apple through a picket fence. Bless your heart."

I can't help laughing at them and it's contagious; they laugh too, and pretty soon we're having a full-blown giggle fit.

"Heyyyy, girls."

It's Emily, Leah, and Maddie in a demented, high pitched chorus. Emily and Leah are in their cheerleading gear, and they don't stop on their way to the rest of the squad for warm ups. Maddie lags behind.

"Y'all wanna come to my house after the game?"

Taylor and Katie exchange glances and say, "No, we can't; we hafta do stuff with our families." It sounds rehearsed, and then they're all staring at me. It takes me a moment to realize that Maddie's invitation includes me, and even though I know that this has been planned, I'm still surprised and flattered.

"Sure!" My own voice sounds strange to my ears, disgustingly enthusiastic. *Whatever happened to the part of me that's proud of being a lone wolf?*

"Cool!" Maddie smiles widely at me and starts walking with us. We move along the sideline, yelling encouragement at the guys. From here, I can see exactly who is worth their time. We stop to talk to Leila, Brittany, and Mandy. We ignore Sarah, Jessie, and Beth, even though they wave madly at us as they pass, just because we can. I feel like I'm in a scene from *Mean Girls*, and self-loathing builds in my gut. The attraction of being included in a group, especially this group, pulls at me—hard—but this is so not me. I'm already trying to figure out a way to bail out of going to the party.

We find a place in the stands by Josh, Tyler, and Brandon, who all give me confused looks. I see their brains running on a treadmill behind their furrowed brows, thinking, *"Wait, didn't they just locker-bomb this chick for like a week straight?"* But they greet me anyway, with a general, delayed mumble of "Hey Flye, how's it going?" and "'Sup Flye?"

I nod back at them and say, "Hey," and wipe my palms indiscreetly on my jeans.

The game starts and everyone's yelling, cheering or booing. I have no idea what the actual rules of football are—another lapse in high school culture that my snobbish family never thought was important enough to teach me. So I never learned to care about sports. I follow Katie and Taylor's lead and yell whenever they yell, faking excitement until I get drawn into it. There's a weird kind of freedom in screaming mindlessly, not being able to hear your own voice in the crowd that's screaming with you. It's like this entire side of the stands is a giant hive-mind, and for once I'm inside of it, consumed and swallowed by the whole.

Still, I don't understand football. It's really nothing more than the Romans and the lions fighting it out in the Coliseum. I mean really, it's just a way for people to vent their pent-up rage and frustration while still maintaining their façade of civilization. I'm over the euphoria of being included in the masses within the first ten minutes. *How much longer is this going to last?*

My smile has become fixed, and my cheeks start to hurt from keeping it up.

I hide a flinch as Katie turns to me, beaming, and asks, "Having fun, Flye?"

I respond with an even bigger smile and say, "Oh, yeah, this is great!"

"Watch Chris. He's just an awesome quarterback. How he moves, how he throws the ball. He's so powerful and graceful..."

I look toward Chris just in time to see two players from the other team dump him on his ass before he can throw the ball. I can't help myself; I laugh out loud, then hastily cover it with a fake sneeze as Taylor, Katie, and Maddie cast astonished looks at me sideways.

"Damn allergies," I shrug.

"Bless your heart," says Maddie.

We win the game 21 to 7. The players on the field have Chris up on their shoulders and they're all soaked in an orange sports drink. My face, legs and back are stiff from smiling and sitting on the cold metal seat, and my throat is aching from so much screaming. Katie, Maddie, and Taylor rise, and I follow them as we join the throng of people leaving the stadium. I contemplate quietly slipping away and heading home, pretending I got lost when they ask about it later, but I'm borne along with the crowd. Once it thins, Katie and Taylor head off together, and Maddie can see my every move, so I'm stuck. Maddie and I walk to her house silently.

Chapter Twenty-Three

The shadows are reaching out to us as we enter Maddie's house through her garage and I shy away as one of the shadows starts walking towards us.

"Jesus, Tommy!" Maddie screams. "You 'bout gave me a heart attack!"

A chunky guy about Stoner's age is carrying a twelve-pack of beer through the door and into the kitchen. He takes a bunch of plastic cups out of a grocery bag and pops open a beer, looking at us with a grin, and says, "Just gotta check the merchandise, make sure my little sis' gets what she paid for."

Maddie laughs and says, "I didn't pay for you to drink it all! Is this all you got?"

"Well yeah, isn't this enough?" I can't tell if he's teasing or serious, but Maddie oozes sugar, deepens her dimples, and pleads, "Please, Tommy, please say you got more than this."

Tommy laughs and says, "Hold on, I'll be right back."

And he is, carrying sodas and several bottles of flavored vodka, tequila and rum. He laughs again and says, "Jesus, Maddie, this is enough to get the Navy drunk. How many people you expectin'?"

"Just my friends," she purrs and then yells, "We won! It's time to CEL! UH! BRATE!"

"Well, you better make sure you clean up all the celebration before Mom and Dad get home tomorrow or it's your ass that'll be on the line, not mine." He smiles at her to take the sting out of his words.

Maddie says sweetly, "Thanks Tommy, I owe you."

He smiles back. "Yes, you do—$74.83, to be exact." He pops another beer, takes a long swallow, slips into his car and backs down the driveway. He roars down the street, waving his arm out the window.

Maddie cranks up Katy Perry and starts pouring drinks. "Whaddaya want, Flye?"

I have no idea. I've never really drunk alcohol before except for the sips of champagne my mom lets me have on New Year's Eve, and that doesn't really count.

I shrug nonchalantly, put on my best James Dean look, and say, "I'll have a beer. I like to start light before I hit the heavy stuff later on."

Where the hell did that come from? I guess it worked though, because Maddie looks surprised and then hands me a cup that looks like it's more foam than beer. She turns toward the door as Chris, Danny, Matt, Emily, Cammie and Leah all walk in. There are hugs and high fives and a lot of yelling and shrieking, before Maddie herds us all into the kitchen where she lines up shots of tequila for everyone. They all yell, "TO-KILL-YA!" before downing the little paper cups of liquid that smells a lot like gasoline, their faces twisting into grimaces and then grins, and everyone—except me—high fives again.

"C'mon, Flye," Leah says as she slams her cup on the counter, daintily wiping her lips with her right pointer finger. "Your turn."

"Nah, I've still got beer," I say, with false bravado, lifting my cup as I turn away, and pretending to take a swallow.

"Yeah, Flye saves the hard stuff for later, after she's caught a beer buzz," Maddie says admiringly, and the Belles and the Jokes look at me with bewilderment. I smile and say nothing as Chris and Emily do another shot, each holding the other's cup and tipping it up, up, up, until there's tequila dripping down Emily's full bottom lip. Chris tries to kiss it away, but Emily stops him with one elegant finger to his chest and then proceeds to slow dance with him. Someone has turned the lights down, and I can see Matt and Maddie making out in the corner while Leila and Danny are grinding with wild abandon next to Chris and Emily. I watch Chris slip his hand lower and lower on Emily's back until she reaches behind her and hikes it back up to her waist with a scolding smirk on her face. He starts doing it again not two seconds later. Leah and Cammie are sitting on the floor, taking long, alternating sips from a bottle of green apple vodka, smacking their lips after every drink. Their laughter gets louder and louder, and whatever conversation they think they're having disintegrates into giggles every couple of minutes. I'm invisible, cradling my untouched beer in both palms and watching the show around me. They're all buzzed, living in their own fuzzy worlds, and I'm no longer an oddity to them. It's funny how when other people are drunk they assume you are too.

Just as I'm wondering how much drunker they need to get before they won't notice if I sneak out, Leah starts chanting "TP, TP, TP!" Leila and Danny pick up the chant, and even Matt and Maddie come up for air to join in as Emily tears off to the bathroom, but I don't hear the sounds of retching that I expected. She comes back with armfuls of toilet paper and starts tossing rolls to the crowd. She lobs one at me, and I reluctantly catch it, holding it like it might bite me.

She laughs and says, "C'mon, Flye. Give it your best shot!"

"Yeah, we hear you're really coooool, " Leah and Maddie drawl out as they laugh drunkenly, slapping each other on the back.

"C'mon Flye," Cammie holds out the bottle of tequila, "have a little liquid courage."

Chris joins her, saying, "Yeah Flye, you're *fly* enough for this, aren't you?" He sways on his feet, leering and winking at me.

Emily glares at him and then runs a long, manicured nail up the side of his neck, drawing his attention away from me. I can see their tongues entwine, and I look away, repelled.

Matt and Danny laugh, "Yeah, Flye, for someone's who cool enough to carry her liquor the way you do, TP'ing Mrs. Meercamp's house will be nothing..."

Emily walks toward me imperiously, but the effect lessened by her tripping over her high heels and falling to her knees. I take another fake drink to hide the laughter on my face.

"C'mon Flye, show us what you're made of. If you want to be one of us, then you hafta do what we do." She ends with a definitely unladylike burp.

Oh. My. God. I can't TP her house. Mrs. Meercamp, who's so nice to me, who wants me to be on the Cameo *staff, who cares about me, who talks about me with Mr. Lester, always trying to do her best for me. I can't be part of this.*

My fear must show because Matt gets up in my face and sneers, "Whatsa matter wif the wil' baby, too scared to party with the big kids? Does widdle baby hafta run home to her mama? You're not so smart now, are ya?"

They've turned on me in a heartbeat like a pack of rabid wolverines, and it all comes rushing into ice cold reality as I finally get it. This is all a set up. They planned this whole thing. Taylor and Katie were part of it from the beginning, gaining my trust and sucking me in. Pain stabs me somewhere around my heart, and for just a second I'm ready to cry before the rage, hot, red and unrelenting, takes over. *Well, guess what bi-atches, I am smarter than all of you put together. Watch this.*

I stagger to my feet as if I'm as drunk as they are, put on my who-the-hell-do-you-think-you-are face, and slur, "Seriously? TP'ing is for amateurs. Don't y'all have some spray paint?"

They stand there in shocked silence, mouth breathing, and then Chris says, "Isn't spray painting someone's house like, uh, I dunno, a felony?"

"Only if you get caught." I sway on my feet, swallow air and belch from the bottom of my toes.

"Oh shit, man, get her outa here, she's gonna hurl," Maddie yells. "Flye, can you hear me?" She's in my face and I almost do hurl from the stench of vodka on her breath. "Come to the bathroom with me. You can't puke on my parents' carpet."

"I'm totally fine, I'm not gonna puke!" I push her out of the way and head to the kitchen. They watch me in stunned, blurry admiration as I grab a shot glass, fake-pour vodka in it, and, holding it cupped in my fist, tilt my head back and "slam" it down. "Ah!" I sigh loudly and wipe my mouth with the back of my hand. "Spray paint?" I look at them with all the contempt I have for them and their kind.

Matt runs into the garage, comes back with a can, shakes it in the air, and yells, "LET'S DO IT," and they're all following me out of the house. They're lined up behind me, staggering, and I grin wickedly into the sweet night air.

Chapter Twenty-Four

We run through the night, down the small-town streets, and I have no clue where we're going. My heart is pounding in rhythm with my feet, and my head is repeating, "What do I do now?" over and over in the same rhythm, but changes to "Oh, God, oh, God, please get me out of this," as we continue farther on. Emily is now in the lead and we finally end up in front of a graceful old Victorian house near Main Street. We stop, panting, our heads bowed and our hands on our knees. The house is dark except for a night-light glowing in the middle of the house. Mrs. Meercamp isn't home.

Oh God, what do I do now? I can't believe I got myself into this mess just because I wanted to belong to a group of idiotic, drunken, wannabe delinquents. I slide unobtrusively into a clump of crepe myrtle bushes, hoping I can just hide.

I glance at the Belles and the Jokes, who are already flinging toilet paper onto the trees in the front yard, and see Chris take a long pull off a vodka bottle while Danny shakes the spray paint can and gets ready to write some obscenity on the dark side of the house. I snort derisively. *Who does he think he is, some small town gangsta, gonna tag an old lady schoolteacher's house with his moniker?*

I pull out my phone, dial 9-1-1, and say, "I need to report some drunken teenagers vandalizing a house at 2285 South Paula Street. Please come right away."

They all start yelling for me. "Flye! Where the hell are you Flye?!" I move toward them just as the back door opens.

"Flye? Is that you, darlin'?" Mrs. Meercamp is there, looking at me wonderingly. "I thought I heard your voice. What's going on out here?"

"Oh my God, Mrs. Meercamp, I'm so sorry. I didn't plan this, I didn't mean for any of this to happen. I just called 9-1-1. I didn't know what else to do."

I trail off as she leads me inside, into the dimly lit kitchen. I hear sirens and see police cars pulling up in front of the house, and the Belles and the Jokes scatter, except they're all too drunk to make it very far. Danny trips over Matt, and they land in a pile, and Emily gracefully slides to the ground in a fake faint. We continue to watch behind the slightly drawn curtains and see Emily, Leah, and Maddie already in handcuffs. Chris projectile vomits all over a policeman's shoes while being handcuffed, and I yelp with laughter. I quickly clap my hand over my mouth, thinking it unseemly to react this way in the presence of a school authority figure, especially one whose house I was supposed to be TP'ing, but the Meerkat is smiling too.

The cops haul all the kids away, lights flashing, sirens blaring, and I sit at the kitchen table in shock, thinking I'm really in deep shit now. Not only do I have a lot of explaining to do to Mrs. Meercamp, but this has just started a war with the Belles and the Jokes that I'll never win. They'll know it was me who called the cops.

I look at Mrs. Meercamp, who puts a warm muffin in front of me and pours me a glass of sweet tea, and I tell her everything that's been going on with these kids, beginning with the first day of school right up to tonight. She listens sympathetically, nodding occasionally.

"I'm so sorry that I was here with them tonight. You must think I'm terrible, doing this to you when you've been so good to me." I can't talk anymore; I'm crying too hard.

"You didn't do anything wrong," she says. "You called the police, which saved me the trouble of doing it."

"You knew they were out there?"

"Sugar, I've been teaching for thirty-five years. This isn't my first rodeo." She hands me a tissue and laughs again. "Besides, they were making so much noise, I think the whole neighborhood heard them. I must say though, I was surprised to see you with them."

I hang my head in shame as fresh tears flow. Finally I ask, "Will they go to jail?"

"No, I won't press charges. I don't want to turn them into criminals. I just want to give them a good scare." She shakes her head and laughs ruefully. Unbelievable! I never thought teachers could be so cool.

"However, young lady," she fixes me with a look of mock sternness, "you do owe me a favor."

Oh, God, now what?

"I want you here tomorrow morning at nine sharp."

What, she wants me to bring a ladder and get all the toilet paper out of her trees?

"Sure, uh, I'll be glad to."

Well, that's not true, but what else can I say? It might have been better if I'd been arrested too.

Chapter Twenty-Five

Mom drops me off at Mrs. Meercamp's house and I ring the doorbell, waiting for doom to fall. Even though I didn't drink anything last night, I still feel like I've got a hangover: my eyes are sticky, my head aches and my stomach is doing flip flops like it does right before I throw up. The door opens and I cringe, expecting the worst.

It's Lily, Georgia, Camille, Dexter, and a girl I don't know.

"Hey, girl!" Georgia gushes.

Dexter grabs my hand and pulls me inside. "C'mon in. We thought you could use a little group therapy."

"And if that doesn't work," Camille walks into the living room, carrying a plate of brownies, "there's always chocolate!"

The Meerkat sits on the floor with her legs crossed, and the rest of us sprawl on couches, chairs, or throw-pillows. A tall girl with long, black hair, flashing black eyes and an aquiline nose glides across the room and says, with a lilting accent, "Hey. I'm Toni."

"She's Antonia Giovannetta Giordano and she's really an Italian princess incognito," Georgia says as she takes a ginormous brownie. Toni laughs, a sound like crystal wind chimes, and I just stare at this creature who seems so out of place here in this room with mere mortals.

"I'm not royalty, Georgia. My parents are both proctologists. There's nothing royal about what they do." She laughs with self-deprecating humor, and suddenly she's just a human girl again.

Dexter takes a huge bite of brownie and says, around a mouthful of chocolate and nuts, "So, spill, girlfriend! What happened last night?"

I glance at Mrs. Meercamp who just gazes placidly back at me. *What the hell? Now I'm some kind of sideshow display, brought over here to give these kids their vicarious jollies?*

I must look as pissed off as I feel because she says, "Flye had a terrible night, and I thought she could use some moral support. She got herself into a bit of a predicament but she handled it magnificently. I've never seen anyone think on their feet as quickly as you did. I thought this would be helpful. I hope you're not upset with me."

She looks so worried. I shrug and say, "It's gonna be all over school on Monday anyway."

"You don't have to tell us anything you don't want to," Lily says, but she looks at me hopefully. Obviously she wants to know everything too, and now everyone's leaning forward in anticipation, so what else can I do?

"Well, it started with the showdown with the Belles and the Jokes—"

"Who?" Camille leans forward so far she practically falls off the couch, and I explain.

Lily laughs out loud. "That's golden."

I give them a few generic details about the party, like how it was a set up, but I don't want to sound like a whiner.

"That's about it," I finish up. "It wasn't really a big deal. Anyone would've done the same thing."

"Not true," Dexter shouts. "I know plenty of people who would've caved and just gone along with it."

"Yeah, really Flye, you were really brave." Toni is looking at me with admiration.

"High school's hard and being a new freshman is a whole new level." Lily looks at me with sympathy and then at Georgia. "Remember how hard it was for you?"

"Oh my God. I was from New Jersey, and everyone here had known each other practically since kindergarten. I was pretty popular in my old school, and everyone here treated me like pond scum."

"You're not scum, Georgia!" Toni laughs. "You're a rare, precious flower, a water...well not exactly a lily." Everyone laughs. "You're a Georgia peach!"

"Alright, enough." The Meerkat is laughing as hard as everyone else. "This is what happens when you get a bunch of writers in a room: death by metaphor!"

We settle down, suddenly remembering we're in the presence of a teacher.

"No, but really," Toni begins, "high school can be really tough. We've got your back."

"It's what we do." Dexter reaches for another brownie and Camille slaps his hand away. He looks at her haughtily.

She says, "Hey, it's not my fault. You told me not to let you eat a second one."

"Well. That sucks. I'll never ask you to be my watchdog again." He gives her a little hug and sits on his hands.

"Yeah, but really, we do support each other, usually through our writing. You can always come to *Cameo* when the world out there gets too hard." Dexter's liquid brown eyes seem to melt even more when he looks at me.

"And besides," Georgia's dimples deepen, "if bonding with us doesn't work, there's always Camille's way."

I look wonderingly at shy, tiny Camille.

"I write murder mysteries," she explains in her wispy voice. "I've had a couple published. When someone in the world hurts my feelings or whatever, I just put them in my book. I grow their characters and make them who I want them to be." She pauses for effect and laughs. "And then I kill 'em!"

We all dissolve in helpless laughter.

As everyone leaves, giving me hugs or hand slaps, I stand at the door with the Meerkat.

"Thank you so much, you know, um, for last night and, uh, this, this was really nice."

"Think nothing of it, Little Flye Girl." She gives me a hug. "You're very special. Someday you're going to figure that out."

Chapter Twenty-Six

I start walking towards home when my cell beeps: a text. I don't recognize the number, and my heart sinks. It's gotta be one of the Belles. Here we go—the war begins.

The text says, "hey flye its jake do u wanna work on a project with me for the science club"

Okay, so I heard Cody tell Jake he was supposed to join the science club, but I hadn't heard anyone mention me. I think about our awkward moment at the lockers yesterday, and an involuntary smile tugs at my lips, and I text him back.

"yeah, maybe, what're u gonna do?" This is so weird; I already know about the project, but I have to pretend that I don't.

"growing plants... hey can I just call u"

"sure"

My phone starts playing the first few bars of *Gimme Shelter,* and I pick up on the third ring. I don't want to look desperate or anything.

"Hey," he says, and I can hear a shy hesitation in his voice.

"Hey," I say back. Suddenly, "hey" feels like the single most stupid thing that anyone could have possibly said in this moment.

"So, you wanna work with me on my science project?" His words are rushed and, for some unfathomable reason, it's vaguely comforting to know that he's uncomfortable too.

"Well, yeah, um...what're you gonna grow?" I flash back to Cody's screen-saver and wonder if it's pot.

"Tomato plants." I breathe a sigh of relief, and Jake loosens up as he starts to talk about experimenting with the effects that different kinds of fertilizer have. I almost ask him what Cody would think of me joining Jake but I catch myself. I'm not supposed to know this is Cody's idea, but a cloudy plan starts to form in my head: if I work with Jake, I can figure out what Cody really has in mind.

It's easy to be enthusiastic about the project with Jake. He seems genuinely into the experiment, and I almost forget that this hadn't even been his idea in the first place. I tell him about my family's garden, how we grow and can our own vegetables, and how I'm pretty good at it. This whole talking-to-a-guy thing is a lot less terrifying once we're actually talking about something.

"So, you wanna start today?"

The awkwardness hits me again and I stop in mid-breath. *Oh my God. I have to see him, stand next to him, and actually talk to him face to face?* "Uh, well, um, maybe, what do you have in mind...?" I trail off.

Now he sounds uncertain too. "Well, um, my mom can drive us to a nursery, and we can get everything we need. We can work in my garage, uh, there's a good space for growing plants."

Oh, what the hell. After what I did last night, leading the juvie brigade, planting some tomatoes with Jake will be nothing.

"Sure," I say, tapping the leftovers from last night's fake-outgoing-popular-Flye routine.

"Why don't you come over to my house and we'll get started."

He texts me his address, which I put into my phone's map. His house is only a couple of blocks from mine. I text Mom, telling her where I'm going, as I start walking toward his house.

When I get there, his mom drives us to the local nursery where we pick out six tomato plants and some pots. As I'm loading them into the car, Jake pushes over a cart loaded down with bags of fertilizer.

"What do we need all that for?" I exclaim. "We've only got six freakin' plants."

"You can never have too much fertilizer." He grins as he loads them in the trunk, and I think again about Cody saying, "The point is the fertilizer." I just know that Jake and I are part of some grand scheme of Cody's, and it scares me, but I don't know what it is, and I can't prove that it even exists.

When we get back to Jake's house, we unload all the stuff and start setting up our project on a table by a south-facing window. At first, we're pretty quiet, just talking when we have to, like, "Could you hand me a plant," and "Please pass the fertilizer," but after a while we both loosen up.

He tells me how his sister and her husband live on a farm in Illinois, and when he graduates from high school he's going to live with them and help them farm. While he talks, he handles the plants delicately, with gentle, careful fingers. I can totally see him on a farm, planting vegetable gardens and looking after crops. He seems to know what to do instinctively. There's a lull in our conversation for a few minutes, and I see his lips moving while his eyes are trained on the little seedlings.

He's whispering something. "There you go, little guy. Grow big and strong."

He sees me listening and flushes pink, but he starts talking at a normal level. "It helps plants grow if you talk to them."

He sees the look of incredulity on my face and says, "No, really, it's a scientific fact."

"Oh, right! Who do you think you're kidding?"

"No, seriously, it's true. Here's how you do it: grow little plant; grow big and strong so I can eat you! Chomp, chomp, chomp!"

We fall over laughing, and we can't stop. I laugh every time I glance up at Jake, and every time I do, he starts laughing too. Soon my belly hurts, and my cheeks are sore, and tears are running out of my eyes.

A shadow falls over the doorway. "Hey man, what're you doing?" It's Cody. The cure for the common giggle fit.

Jake stops laughing immediately and flushes as he explains. "Flye's gonna help me with the science project. We're just getting started."

For a moment, I'm terrified that I'm going to see Crazy Cody with his cold, dangerous whisper, but he seems fairly normal, although he doesn't look exactly thrilled to see me.

"Well, maybe I should get going," I say to Jake as I rise to get my stuff together.

Cody steps in and says, "Naw Flye, you don't have to go. In fact, I've just been thinking about you."

Oh, God. That can't be good.

He sees the look of curiosity and dread on my face and says, "Yeah, your little party last night is all over my computer."

Before I can say anything, Jake asks, "What're you talkin' about, man?"

"It seems our little friend here is a party animal. She and Emily and Chris and the rest of those douche bags went to Meercamp's house to TP it."

I interrupt him, take a deep breath, and tell both of them my side of the story, starting with how it was a set up with the Belles and the Jokes, with everyone but me drinking at the party, me faking being drunk, leading them to Mrs. Meercamp's house, and then calling the cops. I don't tell them about the Meerkat letting me inside so that I could watch the arrests, and I don't tell them about hanging out with some of the *Cameo* people this morning.

Jake and Cody listen quietly, and when I'm finished, Jake whistles softly and says, "Sounds like they thought they were setting you up, but you really kicked their asses."

Even Cody is looking at me with something akin to respect.

"Yeah, well, the shit's gonna hit the fan at school on Monday," I say. "They're gonna kill me."

"Don't worry about it," says Cody, thoughtfully shaking his head. "It'll be okay."

I look at him in worried disbelief and say, "Yeah. Well, I gotta go."

"Okay, Flye, see you Monday," says Jake.

"Yeah, Flye, see you Monday," Cody mocks him.

As I turn away, I hear Cody's voice, shrill and angry. "What the hell are you doing, man? We can't have anyone else in on this, especially not the little flytrap."

"It's okay man, she's nice, I kinda like her…" Jake's voice trails off as they go inside.

Cody's threats go right over my head, and I grin so hard my face hurts all over again. Jake likes me!

Chapter Twenty-Seven

The phone wakes me at five a.m. I can hear Mom squealing like a teenager, interspersed with "Oh my God," "I can't believe it," and "We'll be there. See you soon."

She tears into my room, not bothering to knock, yelling, "Dad's coming home! Dad's coming home today!"

"Wha—? When?"

"Get up. We've got so much to do."

She tears downstairs, and I can hear the vacuum running. Oh. My. God. It's still dark outside. I stumble into the shower, which helps me wake up, and then tie my hair up into a ponytail though it's still dripping. Throwing on a pair of jeans and a t-shirt, I check out my wall for the latest on Friday's fiasco. Sure enough, there's stuff about me all over the place, including a picture of me that someone's altered to look like a mug shot and a message from Bekkah: "What's going on there?!?!"

I don't feel like diving into it all again with Bekkah, so I hack into Cody's computer instead. There are no obvious changes, but "four-twenty" is all over his search and browser history. That's so crazy. *Well, yeah, but so is Cody.*

He has a few poetry websites bookmarked, which is strange—I never thought Cody would be one to get into poetry much. I check out one of them, and it looks like a site full of generic, depressing high school angst. I'm about to close out of it when one of the pennames catches my eye: RebDoomerII. It's the log-in ID to Cody's computer. Cody's a poet? I read the first poem I find posted under his pseudonym.

> The voices scream and rage,
> Turn the page,
> Act your age,
> Life's a cage,
> Full of rage.
>
> It's time to move,
> Nothing to lose.
> The stench of the Reaper's breath.
> There's only freedom
> In death.

It's not exactly a masterpiece, but knowing that Cody actually, literally, might have voices in his head gives it a different meaning altogether. Freedom in death? I shiver, and I suddenly wish I didn't know anything about Cody at all.

I log off his computer, and it's a sweet relief to start chatting with Bekkah.

LoneSheWolf:	yo, avatar, u there
BekkahsAvatar:	whaddup wolfie
LoneSheWolf:	i'm in deep shit
BekkahsAvatar:	OMG!!!!! NOW WHAT??????
LoneSheWolf:	remember how I told you how katie and taylor were being nice to me?
BekkahsAvatar:	yeah...
LoneSheWolf:	it was all a set up...

I start with the soda can that Leah and the others threw at me after school and go on to the game, the party and calling the cops on the Belles and the Jokes.

BekkahsAvatar:	r u kidding? i'm so proud of you!

Proud of me?! Easy for her to say. I've got bitches on wheels after me, a psychopath on the loose, and she's proud?

LoneSheWolf:	yeah, well, it's my butt on the line tomorrow at school, not yours

BekkahsAvatar:	but you did the right thing
BekkahsAvatar:	and the way you set them up....just brilliant! You really are pretty smart after all, aren'tcha?
LoneSheWolf:	it's not a big deal i just didn't know what else to do

I tell her about meeting the *Cameo* kids at the Meerkat's house and working with Jake on the science project. I don't tell her about how I've been hacking into Cody's computer or about the scary poetry or the possibility that Cody's suicidal.   I especially don't tell her I may have a crush on Jake.

Mom's at my door. "Flye, it's time to go."

I sign off with Bekkah and we're out the door to the airport. We wait by the security check-point, and I'm weirdly tempted to ask Mom for advice about Jake. I mean, that's a fairly normal mother-daughter conversation to have, and she would be thrilled that I was telling her about my life, but I don't know for sure how she'd react.   She might say something ooey gooey like, "Oh, sweetie, do you have your first crush?" Or something annoying like, "You're too young to be thinking about boys." Or she might actually be helpful. You just never know with Mom. I decide to risk it.

"So Mom, when you were my age, did you have a boyfriend? Some guy that you sort of liked?"

I hold my breath. She looks at me curiously, and a quick mix of emotions runs across her face: humor, compassion, regret. It reminds me of when I first asked her what a penis was, when I was in about first grade. She has that same oh-no-my-baby's-growing-up look.

But she recovers quickly and says, "Actually, I did in seventh grade. His name was Jimmy. He had zits and braces and I thought he was just so cute. I couldn't bring myself to talk to him, you know. So my best friend communicated back and forth between us. And we passed notes. We sat together once on a school bus on a class trip. We lasted about two months—a long term relationship."

She smiles nostalgically, waiting to see if I'll ask anything else, but she handled that pretty well, so I decide not to push it.

She starts to ask me something and then jumps forward with a little shriek and runs toward a thin man with streaky hair and a deep tan. It takes me a second to recognize my dad. He's lost weight, and his hair, which is normally just as red as mine, is all bleached out. He sees me walking toward him and grabs me and Mom in a big family hug. I can smell his coconut-lime aftershave. His cheeks are scratchy with a scraggly beard that I'm surprised to see has some grey in it. Was that there when he left? We're all laughing and crying and talking at the same time.

Finally, Dad picks up his carry-on bag, and we head to baggage claim to get the rest of his stuff. Mom and Dad walk in front of me, her with her head leaning on his shoulder, both of them with their arms wrapped around each other, oblivious to everyone else. They look like they have their own little solar system. So what does that make me? An asteroid? Space dust? I walk behind them, alone.

Chapter Twenty-Eight

I lie awake in the dark, thinking about everything that happened this weekend and dreading tomorrow. I see Mr. Lester catching a soda can as it makes a ninety-degree turn in mid-air; I see myself in the Box, hanging on every word I hear and craving more because I can never get enough gossip; I see myself with the Belles at the football game, ignoring perfectly friendly people just because everyone else is doing it; and I see myself leading a bunch of drunken idiots to vandalize the house of the nicest teacher I know. *What's happening to me?*

I fall asleep, but only partly. I dream that I'm dreaming. I can sense someone in the room, coming for me, standing over me, watching me sleep, and I can't move or open my eyes, let alone run. I try to wake up but it's as if I'm covered in lead and there's no breath left in my body. The stranger in my room is breathing in hard little gasps and his breath smells like onions and rotten eggs. I feel like I'm going to throw up, but I can't wake up. Trying to scream, my voice only comes out in a wheeze. No one can hear me. No one can help me.

Screaming one more time, I wake myself up with a short yelp and look around my room. My bedside lamp is still on, throwing the corners into shadows. I'm shaking and covered in sweat, panting. Looking around the room carefully, searching for movement in the corners, and even under my bed, I finally realize: *There's no one here. It was just a dream. Settle down, Flye. You're letting your imagination run away with you again.*

I turn off my lamp and raise the shade over the window above my bed. The quarter moon shines through the leaves of the oak tree outside my room. My constant moon. Watching the moon makes me focus on something predictable. It's the opposite of high school, which is so full of stress and games and rules that change as soon as I think I've figured them out.

My gaze wanders as my mind wanders. There's a little bit of moonlight on the ground, casting a faint shadow of the house and the tree limbs. It's calm and peaceful, and I can feel myself getting sleepy, my eyelids getting heavy. Out of the corner of my eye, there's movement—a disk of light sweeping the ground. I jerk awake, and my heart is thumping loudly in my chest.

There's someone walking around the yard! I sidle over to my other window and look out, but there's nothing but the street light on the corner.

You just imagined it, Flye. You're freaked out from the spooky dream. In the midst of my panic, a name floats around in my head. A ghostly image, a fragmented idea: Cody.

I lie awake for a long time, watching the moon drift through tree branches and clouds, watching it disappear behind the woods.

Chapter Twenty-Nine

I'm purposefully late for school, timing my entrance to English at the exact second the tardy bell is ringing. Even so, I don't escape hateful looks from the Belles and Jokes' side of the room. Matt and Chris. Maddie and Emily. They all glare at me, and I can tell they're out for blood.

I try to be invisible, and when Mrs. Meercamp turns on the projector there's an audible gasp from around the room as a short article from *The Spring Valley Reporter* fills the screen. I scan it quickly, looking for my name.

"Seven teenagers were arrested Friday night at the home of Mrs. Portia Meercamp on charges of vandalism, public intoxication, and underage drinking…" It's like an indictment, and everyone in the room is looking accusingly at me.

Then someone says, "Holy shit! Look at that!" and we're all facing the screen again as the 9-1-1 message is projected under the article. The transcript is exactly what I said with a phone number under it. A phone number that isn't mine.

How can this be? I look around the room in confusion and stop when I see Emily's face. She's looking at Chris like she doesn't recognize him, open accusation and horror in her expression. Chris is pale, like all the blood has suddenly drained from his face.

"You sold us out."

There's venom in Emily's voice that I've never heard before— not a drop of her usual saccharine tone. Chris is shaking his head, but the rest of the Belles and Jokes are looking at him in disbelief and revulsion.

I look at Mrs. Meercamp and she winks discreetly as she returns the class to order.

"Don't worry about it," Cody had said on Saturday, almost reassuringly. I'm stunned. It's Cody, crazy Cody, the kid who has a secret personality and manipulates Jake; the kid who writes terrifying poetry; the kid who just saved my ass for no discernible reason. *Why?*

"Class," the Meerkat says, "we're not going to give this message any time or thought. And as far as what you may have heard about certain incidents Friday evening, that's not up for discussion either. This is English, not some third-rate tabloid, and we're here to work." She turns to the board and starts writing, "Iambic pentameter."

Turning around and seeing most students still talking among themselves, she says sharply, "I expect you to take notes. They will be turned in to me and they will be graded."

The chatter stops amid moans and frustrated mutterings, but everyone does as she asked, and the room is quiet and focused.

Half way into passing period, everyone in the school has learned about Chris's apparent treachery. Emily and Leah come up to me and say, "We know it was you who called the cops, you stupid little bitch."

I cut them off with a contemptuous glare. "In case you don't know, that was the official transcript from a 9-1-1 call that I didn't make because that's not my phone number on it. You know whose number that is."

I turn away and start walking as they stare at me open-mouthed, and then Leah catches up to me, grabs my arm, and gets in my face. "You're a lying little slut," she snarls harshly, spitting in my face.

I shake free from her nasty grip. "Take your hands off me, and don't ever touch me again. That's assault. Do I need to have my parents contact our lawyer? Aren't you in enough trouble as it is?"

They back away, and I swear I see tears of fear in Emily's eyes. I smirk openly in triumph. Other people have gathered around, ready to see the show, and I give them my fiercest don't-screw-with-me face.

A quiet voice says, "Alright, that's enough. Everyone go to class right now or all of you go to detention."

It's Mr. Lester. As the crowd disperses, I see people glancing back at me. But now, instead of open hatred or mocking jeers, I see sparks of curiosity, maybe even respect.

"Are you alright, Little Flye Girl?" Mr. Lester looks at me kindly.

"Yeah," I say, "I'm better than I've ever been."

I look at him and give him the first genuine smile I've had on my face in this school. I high five him and swing down the hall to Geometry.

Everyone's still buzzing about the article and the 9-1-1 message, but Mr. Johnson is a no-nonsense kind of teacher and gets us quiet right away. I glance over at Jake and catch his eye. He smiles and gives me a thumbs-up. I'm so high on my victory in the hallway that I don't even blush, and I give him a thumbs-up too, like we're conspirators in an underground plot. I guess maybe we are.

Jenn can't wait to talk. "Okay, you have to tell me everything. Right now." Under the guise of helping her with a formula, I give her an edited version of the party, telling her about how they were all drunk but leaving out the part where I led them to the Meerkat's house with a can of spray paint.

"So when I knew what their plans were—that they were going to the Meerkat's—I just sneaked away and went home," I finish as she stares at me wide-eyed.

"So did you make the 9-1-1 call?"

"No," I lie. "That's Chris' number on the transcript of the call. You should've seen Emily's face when she saw it up there. She looked like she was gonna to murder him."

Well, at least that's the truth.

"Unbelievable," she murmurs, as Mr. Johnson glances sharply at us, and we scribble nonsense into our notebooks, too preoccupied to concentrate.

"Flye?" Jenn whispers.

"Yeah?" I say, expecting her to need help with a problem.

"Do you want to hang out at my house after school for a while? Evan's gonna be there too."

I look at her questioningly. "Is it okay?" I trail off, wondering if she'll get in trouble with the Belles.

She giggles silently and says, "Well, yeah, who cares about them anymore?"

"Um, yeah, sure."

"Cool," she whispers, and then says, "I don't get number twelve."

We both giggle quietly and put our heads together over her math book.

Chapter Thirty

It's lunchtime in the Box. I barely have time to sit down before I hear Emily, her voice transformed from Southern Belle into something that resembles a brawler in a cat fight.

"That skanky little ho! I'll kill her!" It's Emily like I've only heard her once before, on Friday night. "And you two," she shrieks, and I can practically see her hair frizzing out from her foundation-slathered, apoplectic face, "are pathetic!"

"But, Emily, we just did what you told us to!" It's Katie, and she sounds like she's in tears.

"Yeah, Emily, it's not our fault—" It's Taylor, her voice wavering too.

"It's totally your fault," Emily howls. "Flye was supposed to get in trouble, not us."

"But we didn't do anything wrong," Taylor tries to protest again.

"You did everything wrong! Everything about both of you is wrong! Just get out of my sight. Don't ever come near me again! Don't ever come near any of us again!" The door slams behind her. A moment later, I hear it creak open again.

"What's going on in here? I heard screaming out in the hall." It's Jenn.

Katie and Taylor collapse in tears and I can hear Jenn saying, "Hey, it's okay. Everything's okay. Tell me what's happening..."

Katie starts to tell her about how Emily and Leah got them to be friends with me, but it was all just a set up.

"But she's nice, and we like her," Taylor says.

"And we didn't know what Emily had planned, we just did what she said."

"And we weren't even invited to the stupid party!" Taylor finishes on a wail.

It's quiet for a while, the silence broken only by heartbreaking girl-sobs, and then Jenn says, "Okay, here's what we're gonna do—"

I'm suddenly distracted by voices from another hole in the wall.

"We got 'em good, didn't we Jakey?" It's Cody's voice, sounding relatively normal, coming from my right. He laughs but it sounds happy and light-hearted, not the usual maniacal howl.

"They're all out there fighting among themselves. Some are on Chris's side. Some hate him. The precious little darlins' all have their panties in a wad, and now everyone can see who they really are: a bunch of backstabbing, clueless phonies." He laughs again and this time he sounds a little on the crazy side.

"You did a really good thing for Flye," Jake says softly.

"I didn't do it for the flytrap, you moron. I did it for us, and wait 'til you see what comes next." I'm chilled all over, wondering what else he has planned.

"Yeah but Flye's a nice girl. Just give her a chance." I can't help it. I love it that Jake's standing up for me.

Cody howls again and says in his cold, less-than-human voice, "Oh, I'll give her a chance alright. Just wait."

Jake sighs and says, "C'mon, the bell's gonna ring. Let's go."

The door closes behind him as he leaves, and I start to pack up my stuff to leave too when I hear, "It's time, and you know it. They got the fertilizer, and you can use your cell phone; there's just one more step left—"

It's Cody's crazy voice, chilling me to my bones, and I try to think what he could mean. *Who has the fertilizer? What would he use his cell phone for?*

"Jake's right, she's okay. I don't wanna do this—" Cody is whimpering like a little boy, like I've heard him before, like when he was fighting with himself and unable to stand up to his other personality. It's chilling to hear.

The ice-cold, alien voice continues, "Come on now, Cody. Do what Eric says. You always do what Eric says, don't you, Little Cody?"

Cody's voice quivers with fear and tears and he whispers, "Yes?"

"That's a good boy, Cody. Do what Eric says and everything will be alright." The door closes and the room is empty.

I stay in the Box, shaking and terrified of the sinister threats I've just heard. And who the hell is Eric, and what does he want Cody to do?

You've got to tell someone. Go tell Mr. Lester right now!

And what do I say? That I've been eavesdropping on everyone's conversations, that I'm the snitch of the universe and that I really don't know what, if anything, Cody's planning? I'll tell when I know enough to say something.

I'm still trembling as I walk back upstairs and into the hallway toward my next class. Mr. Lester appears next to me and asks, "Are you okay, Little Flye Girl? You look like you've seen a ghost." He smiles his warm, open smile at me.

Maybe I'm looking at one right now. This guy makes some seriously uncanny appearances.

"Yeah, I'm okay, Mr. Lester, just a little distracted is all."

He looks at me sympathetically and says, "Don't worry. Everything's alright."

Chapter Thirty-One

Jenn stops by my locker after school. "Wanna walk to my house together?"

"Um, actually, I have to stop by Mrs. Meercamp's room for a couple minutes. She wants to talk to me about *Cameo*. I'll just catch up to you."

"Well, okay." She gives me her address and looks at me with concern. "You're not in trouble are you, you know, with her house Friday night and all?"

"Oh, no. She just wants to go over some submissions and stuff."

"Well, okay. See you later." She glances over her shoulder at me with another worried look as she walks out the front door.

Glancing around, I head downstairs for the Box. I just want to see if I can hear any more from Cody and figure out what he's planning.

Oh yeah, right. You're such a gossip junkie, you can't stay away from this place for more than a couple of hours.

That's not true. I'm just trying to figure out what's up with Cody.

Oh for God's sake. Just admit it. You're an addict.

School has emptied out quickly and there's not a sound down here. I listen for a few minutes and am ready to leave when I hear the sound of soft music coming off to my left. It's Mr. Schwartz's room and I can hear the sound of a pen scratching on paper. Maybe he's actually grading papers? What a shock.

There's the sound of a bottle opening, liquid splashing against ice and the thud of glass on wood. Is he drinking in there? At school?

I think about hearing Evan and Dusty finding a bottle of liquor hidden in Gimli's room and the talk I heard between Schwartz and Brauer. It was only last week but after the weekend I had, I'd forgotten all about it. I imagine Schwartz sitting at his desk in the slanting afternoon light, drinking whiskey and listening to his pathetic light jazz, thinking it makes him seem cool, because he doesn't have anywhere else to go.

Chapter Thirty-Two

I knock at Jenn's door and she's there right away, with a big smile, inviting me in and offering me a soda. Evan's in the kitchen and we greet each other. It's awkward, I realize, because I know him a lot better than he knows me and he has no idea. I guess it's one of the hazards of the Box, my knowing more about people than they realize, so I can sometimes tend to act like I know them better than I actually do. And that's where it gets awkward.

Jenn pours chips into a bowl and Evan sets out some salsa dip as the doorbell rings. Jenn runs to the door and comes back with Katie and Taylor.

What the hell? What're they doing here? They got me sucked into this mess in the first place! Is this another set-up?

My thoughts must show on my face because Jenn says, "Flye, I really did want to hang out with just you and Evan, but then I talked with Katie and Taylor today, and I thought it would help if—"

Taylor cuts her off. "We're so sorry, Flye, for what we did to you."

Katie jumps in. "We didn't know what Emily and Leah had planned."

"We really thought they wanted you to be a part of our group. I mean, their group."

"They just used us, too—"

"We're so sorry, we really like you—"

Their words tumble together as I look at their scared faces skeptically and remember how much fun we had at the mall and how nice they were to me. They couldn't have been completely faking that, could they? And I remember, on that day, I liked them too.

My resolve to hate them fades and I look at them with the beginning of a smile. "It's okay. I know how they are, and I know you didn't mean it." *Well, that's sort of the truth. Besides, if Jenn trusts them, I guess I can too.*

They both laugh, wipe away tears, and hug me.

"Okay, okay." Evan is laughing too, separating us. "Don't go all emo now."

"Okay. You're not gonna believe this! Guess what I heard today?" Taylor's voice ratchets up to a screech.

"Spill." Evan's all over it.

"I heard..." drawing out the suspense as long as she can, widening her eyes and looking at each of us, "that..."

"Oh for God's sake, Taylor, just say it."

"Okay, okay, I heard that Chris and Danny and Matt have been suspended from football and all extracurricular activities and—"

"—and the same thing happened to Emily and Leah." Katie finishes for her. "They've been kicked outta cheerleading. And Leila and Maddie are suspended from volleyball."

"NO! WAY!"

"YEAH! WAY!"

"So now there're two openings on the JV cheerleading team and they're holding tryouts tomorrow. Hey Flye," Katie laughs, "wanna try out?"

"Hey, yeah!" Taylor yells. "Let's all try out! Talk about karmic payback!"

We all collapse in laugher and I can't believe what's happening. No one here is mad at me; in fact, they like me. I have friends. Evan is watching me and as our eyes meet, he smiles. I grin right back.

"Well, the Belles and the Jokes," I begin, ready to start really gossiping about them. Everyone's looking at me in confusion just like the *Cameo* kids did on Saturday. I flush a little, remembering that it wasn't long ago that my new friends were all included in these disparaging labels.

"The 'Belles' is what I call all the popular, uppity girls and the 'Jokes' are the guys, you know, the Jocks, only Jokes." I trail off, hoping I'm not offending them. I mean, I just got these friends; I don't want to blow it now.

They all look at me in silence for a moment, and then everyone bursts into laughter.

"Oh. My God." Katie shrieks. "That's the funniest thing since...since..."

"Twerking?" Evan finishes for her.

"Oh God, they're worse than that will ever be!" Taylor yells.

We all fall over laughing again. I have a stitch in my side, and I start to hiccup, which makes everyone laugh even harder.

Katie brings me a glass of water. "Here, drink this upside down."

I try to follow her directions but end up pouring it all over my face and clothes, and the laughter reaches near-hysteria. We laugh until we're limp messes, hanging on our chairs, and then Jenn raises her soda can in mock solemnity.

"To the Belles and the Jokes," she says. "Long may they—"

"—rip each other new ones." Evan finishes for her and we all click our sodas together and drink deeply.

Evan is looking at me, but says to everyone, "Hey, we should all go to Homecoming together this Friday."

"Yeah!"

Katie and Taylor are all over it, and before I can say anything, we're making plans to go shopping at the mall tomorrow.

We all leave as the sun starts to set, calling out "Bye," and "See ya tomorrow!" Jenn impulsively gives me a little hug, and Evan and I high five as I start walking toward home, skipping on my shadow and humming *Dog Days Are Over*.

My phone bleeps: I have a text.

It's from Jake.

"do u want to go to homecoming with me?"

As if this day couldn't get any better! I'm ready to text him back when my phone bleeps again.

"ur day is coming u dumb bitch. eric"

Chapter Thirty-Three

I race home, totally forgetting about Jake, Homecoming, and everything else, and slam into my room and search "Eric" on my laptop. I get hits for a library search engine and some sites for baby names. Nothing is making sense. I hack Cody's laptop; he's been visiting poetry pages and writing more bad poetry, but that's about it.

I search RebDoomerII and I freeze as I scan the sites that come up. They're all about the Columbine shootings in Colorado and the killers, Dylan Klebold and Eric Harris.

Oh my God. *Eric...*

I pull my comforter around me and read on, mesmerized. The shooters were bullied. They had social problems. They were labeled losers and misfits. They built pipe bombs in a garage, and no one knew about it until, on April 20, 1999, they came to school armed with the bombs and with guns. They killed students and a teacher, and injured others. Then they killed themselves.

People found out later that they published their bombing plans online. They had many references to killing and violence, and Eric Harris kept a diary of all the events leading up to the massacre. And no one knew about it until it happened. How could that be? How could no one know, not even their parents? That was pretty much the community's reaction too—people blamed the parents. I guess that's what happens. Someone has to be at fault. But those parents lost their children too. It doesn't make sense.

I think about what I've heard Cody say to Jake about what's coming next. I think about his "Crazy Cody" side and how he seems like he's capable of anything. And I think about Jake, buying all that fertilizer because Cody told him to. Is he really all that gullible, or does he know more than he lets on? I've only heard snippets of their conversations, but there could be much more to their plans than what I've heard.

I think about searching "How to make a pipe bomb," but I'm afraid to. Afraid of what I'll find. Afraid of who might find me. If you use the Internet to find out how to build a bomb, can you get arrested for being a terrorist?

I watch the moon, now almost full, drifting through the clouds, and can find no answers or comfort, so I plug into my ear buds and blast Jimi Hendrix's *All Along the Watchtower*.

"There must be some kind of way out of here,

Said the joker to the thief.

There's too much confusion, I can't get no relief...

All along the watchtower..."

Life is not a joke, everything is confusing and there's no way out. I've made up my mind. Tomorrow I tell Mr. Lester everything I know about Cody.

Chapter Thirty-Four

I get to school early and look around for Mr. Lester, but I can't find him anywhere. The Box beckons when I walk down the basement steps, and I enter it silently, grateful for a brief respite from my chaotic life. Although lately, it's been adding to the chaos rather than relieving it.

There are voices coming from the office, and I listen.

"Come in and sit down, Chuck." Mr. Brauer sounds angry.

"Whassup, Bob?" It's Gimli, but he sounds different. His words are a little slurred, and I can hear him stumble a little when he sits down. Oh my God. Is he drunk?

"How much have you had to drink today?"

"Nothing! I haven't been drinking! I swear I hardly ever drink. I would never come to school drunk." He giggles a little. This is surreal.

"You're lying. I can smell it on your breath. And one of the custodians found a bottle of bourbon in your room yesterday. How long has this been going on?"

"What? I don't know what you're talking about." Mr. Schwartz is raising his voice in anger now, sounding a lot like he does in class when he's picking on one of the kids he doesn't like: mean, sarcastic, baiting.

"Chuck. Your breath is about to knock me over. You're falling down drunk."

Gimli starts to protest again, but Brauer takes a deep breath and continues. "You have two choices here. If you're honest with me, I can arrange for you to have a leave of absence, go to a rehab center, a Twelve Step program, whatever it takes for you to get well. Then, hopefully, you can come back here. If you continue lying, I'll make sure you never teach again. It's your choice."

"You can't do that. You don't have that kind of power. You just think you do. I'll teach wherever I want to."

"You'll need references, and you can count on me not giving you a good one. I'll tell the truth. Not just about the drinking, but about what a poor teacher you've become." I can tell Mr. Brauer isn't kidding and Schwartz must know it too.

There's silence. Gimli clears his throat and blows his nose.

Brauer tries again. "C'mon, Chuck. I'm going out on a limb for you here, partly because we've been friends a long time, and partly because I know there's still a good teacher somewhere deep inside of you. I want to give that teacher a chance. What do you say?"

Gimli starts to talk. His voice is barely a whisper and I can hardly hear him. "It started after Linda left me. Oh hell, that's not true. It started a long time ago. That's why she left me. I've known it's been a problem for a long time now. I just thought I could control it. I swear to you, this is the first time I've come to school drunk."

I think about hearing him in his room after school, when we both thought no one else was in the building, when I thought I heard something being poured over ice in a glass. A year ago, even a month ago, I would have been disgusted and just plain grossed out at what he's been doing. Now, I just feel sad for him—all the lonely, screwed up people like him and Cody. And maybe even me, lurking around in the basement shadows like some kind of Quasimodo, feeding on other people's secrets, hiding from my own life.

I turn my attention back to the conversation. Mr. Brauer is calling Mr. Dickenson, asking him to come to the office. When he gets there, Brauer asks Mr. Dickenson to take Schwartz home. "I want you to take a couple of sick days. I'll be in touch this afternoon, and we'll work out a plan to get you some help," he says to Schwartz.

The door to the office closes, and I sit there in the warm silence. Is anything ever what it appears to be?

Chapter Thirty-Five

Jake is hanging out by my locker, looking sheepish, and it takes me a second to even recognize him since I've been living in this alternate universe called the Box, where hidden truths are reality. Now I have to morph into my "real" life.

"Hey Flye," he says, barely making eye contact. He looks so sweet and innocent, so normal, that I'm convinced he can't possibly know anything about what Cody might be up to.

I smile, getting up the nerve to actually look at his face from this proximity and say, "Hey Jake."

"Do you want to come over to my house after school and work on the tomatoes? I thought we could take some measurements and start a spread sheet."

The Great Unspoken Question lies between us, so palpable that it practically has solid form. I decide to take some of the pressure off, so I say, "Sure that would be great. And about Homecoming—"

Jenn, Evan, Katie, and Taylor all come rushing over to me. Oh my God. Talk about timing.

"Flye, remember we're going to the mall after school today to get dresses for Homecoming?"

I screw up my face at her so she can catch on to the fact that she's interrupting, but Jake is already backing away, mumbling, "See you after school."

His face is dark with disappointment, his shoulders slump, and I'm reminded of the first day of school when I saw him being attacked by the Belles and the Jokes; I can't do the same thing to him.

"Jake, wait a sec," I call after him. He looks up blankly, expecting nothing. "I'd love to go to Homecoming with you, but these guys asked me first. Would it be okay if we all go together, you know, kind of as a group?"

I look hopefully around at him and the rest of them, waiting for reactions. Jake smiles happily, and Jenn, Evan, Katie and Taylor are all nodding enthusiastically.

"Cool!" Evan says. "We better get to class."

We all walk down the hall together, ignoring looks from the Belles and the Jokes, laughing just because it feels good. We arrange the shopping trip for later, after Jake and I work on science club together, and a thought occurs to me.

"Where's Cody today?" I ask Jake.

"He's sick."

You have no idea.

Mrs. Meercamp watches Jake and me walk into English with a little smile and nod, and turns to the projector. Class begins.

Chapter Thirty-Six

"C'mon, Flye, let's go eat lunch!" Evan and Jenn are waiting for me at my locker. They notice me glance at Jake over by the window, and Evan calls out, "Hey, Jake, wanna eat lunch together?"

"Yeah, sure," says Jake, and we all head into the cafeteria. I glance around nervously at the Jokes' and Belles' table; Leah and Chris sneer at me sideways, but the rest just ignore all of us. Katie and Taylor already have a table at the back near some of the theater and music crowd, and we open lunch bags. I notice Jake doesn't have a lunch and wonder if he ever eats anything at school. I've only seen him hanging out with Cody, playing video games or helping him with his reading.

I say, "I packed way too much if anyone wants some of this," pushing a banana and a bag of chips toward the center of the table, but more towards Jake.

"Yeah, me too," says Katie, adding a candy bar and a bottle of juice to the pile.

"So I hear Gimli's out sick today," says Taylor, feigning sympathy but smiling delightedly. "Poor baby..." she trails off as the rest chuckle contemptuously.

"Yeah, I heard there's a cool sub," says Jenn. "Maybe we'll actually learn something today."

"Don't count on it," says Evan.

I just sit and listen, struck again with the thought that I've been living such a parallel life all this time in the Box. I know why Gimli's not here, but the rest of them probably never will. A bittersweet regret washes over me, remembering the quiet comfort of sitting in the corner of the Box, hearing voices spill their secrets, feeling like I was on the inside but also being more of an outcast than ever. I look around the table at my new friends, laughing, gossiping harmlessly about Schwartz and making plans for Homecoming and a warm infusion of happiness and contentment enfolds me. So this is what it feels like. Skipping a grade might have been worth it after all.

After school, Jake is waiting for me outside, and we're walking to his house when a tan SUV pulls up next to us. We both shy a little to the side, a by-product of the terminally bullied who are always waiting for the next catastrophe. Jake recognizes the car as Cody leans out and says, "Yo, Jake. Want a ride home?" Then he looks at me and says, "You too, Flye."

I look at Jake, not sure what to say, but Jake says, "Sure," and hops in, leaving me to climb in the backseat with him. Cody's mom says hi to Jake and that they came by school to get Cody's homework, and Jake says, "This is Flye."

"Hello, Flye, it's always nice to meet Cody's friends." *Well, that's pushing it, but whatever.* I suddenly remember that I didn't talk to Mr. Lester today like I had promised myself I would. Oh well, I'll do it tomorrow. Maybe.

We drive down the street while Jake says, "So you feeling better?"

"Not really. Think I can stay home again tomorrow, Mom?" Cody looks hopefully at his mom with his pale eyes and coughs. It sounds real, a deep, hacking sound from the bottom of his lungs, and she places her wrist on his forehead with a worried frown.

"Well, you do feel a little warm, honey, but I won't be able to stay home with you. Let's see how you feel tomorrow."

"Yeah, whatever," he says with a combination of amusement and frustration.

I listen silently, amazed at how normal Cody seems. Have I been imagining the conversations Cody's had with himself? Or how about the times he's been so mean and hateful to Jake?

Cody's mom pulls into Jake's driveway and Cody says, "Later, man," to Jake and "See ya, Flye," to me. We go into the garage, and Jake exclaims, "Holy crap!" looking at about twenty PVC pipes stacked in the corner.

He sticks his head in the back door and yells, "Mom! I'm home," and his mom comes out a few minutes later with sodas and cookies. Jake says, "What's that all about," motioning towards the pile of pipe.

"Oh, who knows? Probably some project your father's working on. You know how he is. I don't ask and he doesn't tell."

She looks at me, startled, as if she's just realized that I'm standing here and says, "Oh, hello, Flye. How are you, darlin'?"

"I'm fine, ma'am, how're you?"

"Oh, just peachy," she smiles and offers us cookies. "Are y'all working on the tomatoes today?"

"Yes, ma'am," I say, and we chat a little more about school and Homecoming, and then she's back in the house, and we're alone with the plants.

There's an awkward silence and then I ask, "So how does Cody feel about me working with you on this project?"

He looks surprised and says, "Okay. Why?"

"I dunno, I just get the feeling that he doesn't like me."

"Nah, Cody likes you."

"Is he going to Homecoming?"

Jake looks at me incredulously and says, "No, why would he do that?"

"I dunno, I just wondered..." This is getting more awkward by the second, so I search frantically for another subject.

"I started the spreadsheet for the data," I begin.

Just as he says, "So where do you want to start?"

We both blush, fake laugh awkwardly, glancing away and then accidentally making eye contact so that we both blush even more.

I take a breath and try to act like a normal human being. "How 'bout we measure the height of the plants now, I'll record them on the spreadsheet, and then we give them some fertilizer and I'll record that data too. Then next time, we can just repeat the whole process."

Jake looks relieved and says in a rush, "Yeah, great idea, let's just measure the fertilizer...uh, I mean, the plants...whatever. What you said."

We work together silently for a few minutes as the tension between us dissipates.

Jake says, "I think Homecoming will be fun."

"Yeah, me too. I hope it was okay that I invited Jenn and Evan and everyone else."

"Yeah, it's fine." The relief of not having to be alone together for a whole night shimmers visibly in the air around us.

I look up suddenly, feeling a change in the atmosphere, and there's Cody, just hanging out by the garage as he smiles at both of us and says, "Well, look at the little scientists, working their butts off." He chuckles a little. "I'm sure those tomatoes are gonna love you guys forever." He seems friendly, but his pale, expressionless eyes stare at me for a second, and chills run up my arms. I shiver involuntarily and hug myself for warmth.

Jake doesn't seem to notice anything. "Hey, Cody, we're just finishing up, and I got the new 3D chess game. Wanna check it out?"

Just then my ride pulls up (what perfect timing), and I say, "Gotta go, see ya," to Jake and rush past Cody without looking at him. I pile in the back seat with Taylor and Katie as we head off to the mall, with everyone chirping away like a bunch of baby chickens. I glance out the window. Jake is opening the door and going inside but Cody is watching me, his reptilian eyes passive and inscrutable. Our eyes meet, and he smiles his bland, normal-kid smile and turns away.

Chapter Thirty-Seven

We're in the junior department, and I'm trying on dresses, looking for something that doesn't make me look too much like a nine-year-old princess.

Everyone's talking at once. "You need something short to show off your cute legs—"

"Here, try this, it's got a high neck with a lot of little pleats. It'll make you look like you've got boobs."

"I've got nothing."

"Yeah, but you will. I was built like two BB's on a board until last year."

"Maybe you should get a padded bra."

"Yeah, that might work."

"I already have one; it was a gift, remember?"

Everyone's quiet for a minute. God, what a buzzkill I can be. Then they laugh, and I join in, and I say, "Maybe I should wear that one."

"Then you'll look like a ho."

"Yeah, a nerdy ho."

By this time a saleslady is looking at us, walking over and saying, "Girls, may I be of assistance?" We tone it down and get serious.

Later, as we all carry our bags out of the store, Jenn says, "Flye, you need a new hairstyle, girl. You look like you've been raised in a jungle."

"Oh, yeah," laughs Katie, "and I know just the person to do it." We walk over to *Hair Today* and before I know it, I'm sitting in a chair with Magritte, my stylist from France, who's cutting my hair so short, I think I'm going to be bald. There's more hair on the floor than there is on my head. I close my eyes, terrified to see the end result, but Taylor says, "Oh. My. God. That's so cute!"

"Oh, yeah, it's great!"

"C'mon, Flye, look in the mirror! You're gonna love it!"

I open my eyes cautiously, one at a time, and there I am, barely recognizable, but looking pretty good. Actually, kind of cute. Almost pretty.

Everyone is gathering around me, exclaiming over my makeover and Jenn says, "Okay, just one more thing," and we're getting manicures. My nails are painted pale lavender with yellow flowers. I just sit back and marvel. *Girly things can be fun. Who knew?*

Jenn's mom drops me off at my house just as the sun is setting, and Mom and Dad have supper ready as I walk in the kitchen, hand her the credit card she let me borrow, and am about to say thanks when she screeches.

"Oh my God! You cut off all your hair!" She looks horrified, but then her expression subtly changes from dislike to contemplation and finally settles on pleasure. "I like it!" she declares. *Well, good, because I can't put it all back.*

They both want to see what I bought, so I model my new dress and shoes, turning dramatically in a wide circle. Mom is beaming, but Dad has tears in his eyes.

"What's wrong? Don't you like it?" I ask him.

"Nothing," he says, wiping at his eyes. "You're beautiful. You're all grown up. How did this happen? You were just born last week..." He trails off in bewilderment.

It happened when you weren't here, I want to lash out at him, but I bite my tongue. *It's not his fault his job takes him away from home, and it's not my fault I'm growing up. It's just what we both do.*

I go up to my room to change for supper and catch a glimpse of myself in the mirror. The dress is a soft, shiny, greenish-gold that brings out the flecks of green in my hazel eyes, which look bigger with my new fluffy curls framing my face. The hem of the dress just brushes the tops of my knees. My legs, which look less coltish and more willowy, end in a pair of green heels. *I guess I'd better learn how to shave my legs.* I take a couple of steps back, and my ankles buckle. *This is gonna take some practice. I can't even walk in these things; how the hell am I ever gonna dance in them?*

173

And then I realize that I have no idea how to dance. What do people even do at high school dances? My only experience is the drunken bumping and grinding that the Belles and the Jokes did at Maddie's party, and a sixth grade fiasco where all the boys stood on one side of the room and the girls stood on the other, whispering, pointing, and pretending to know what they were doing.

My new friends will dump me, and my social life will be over before it even starts. I'll be a loser forever. I'm gonna die.

Okay Flye, get a grip. You can search "how to dance" and try to figure something out.

I start hanging up my dress and putting away my shoes. There's a light knock on the door. It's Mom. She gives me a little hug and says, "You look so pretty, with your hair and nails and everything..." She looks around nervously and I know this isn't what she came up here to talk to me about.

She clears her throat and says, "I'm so glad you're making friends and fitting into high school. I was really worried about you for a while; you seemed so lonely and miserable, and I thought maybe we made a mistake, having you skip eighth grade."

Seriously? She was worried about me? And, maybe she made a mistake? Ya think? I go to say something mean and sarcastic but change my mind in mid-thought. I mean really, what's the point? What's done is done.

Instead, I say, "It's okay, Mom. It was a big adjustment at first, but I'm doing okay."

Except that Cody is a psychopath and is probably planning God-knows-what, but I can't tell anyone, and up until a couple of days ago my main social activity was listening in on everyone else's lives in a hidden room that might be some kind of magic box, and—oh yeah—let's not forget the party-from-Hell last Friday night, after which the aforementioned psychopath actually saved my ass from being the pariah of the entire school, but hey, no biggie, life is good.

"Are you sure?" Tears are balancing on her eyelids, threatening to jump. "Because I can get you back into middle school if you want me to."

This is so typical Mom, blind as a mole and clueless to boot. Of course she would offer to send me back to middle school on the very day that it seems I've finally made some friends, and am going to Homecoming, and doing all the normal high school stuff that she's been wanting me to do.

"Mom, really, it's okay. You were right. I have been more challenged in high school, the work is harder, the teachers expect more..." I'm running out of reasons to make her feel better. I swear, sometimes I feel like the adult, and she seems like the child.

"Really?"

"Yeah Mom, really." I give her a little sideways hug as we walk downstairs together.

Chapter Thirty-Eight

Cody's back. He looks terrible: paler than ever and sort of shrunken. Hardly anyone notices him at the lockers, and he hangs around Jake like a homeless child on a cold winter day. I walk to morning classes with Jenn, Evan, Taylor, and Katie, but I notice that Jake doesn't join us. He's busy with Cody, and I feel sorry for him. He's like a single parent with a very needy kid.

I fake an excuse to get out of lunch with my friends and head for the Box for the first time this week. I can't believe how much I've missed it and can't wait to sit in my comfy corner, listening to the news of the day. Voices are starting as I walk in, so I flop on the floor and tune in.

"I love you, Chris. I'll always love you. Please don't ever leave me." It's Emily.

"I love you too, Em. How could I not love you? We're the couple that everyone else wants to be. I'm not going to leave that. I mean, leave you... I'm not going to leave you, babe."

Oh, barf.

"I don't know..." Emily sounds scared and whiny. "After the party and everything, you know, getting kicked out of football and cheerleading, we've just lost so much, and we're not even as popular as we were. I don't know. Everybody hates me!" It's a long, drawn-out wail. "Please promise me you won't leave me too. Please!" Her sobs are coming harder now, with little hiccups and gasps for air.

Chris is freaking out. "Em, it's okay. Don't go getting all emo on me. This is just a phase. Everyone will forget about...you know. I can't believe they all think I made that phone call. We know it was that little pain-in-the-ass Flye. I don't know how she changed that message, but she did. She'll get hers."

I laugh silently. *Yeah, right. Doesn't appear to be happening.*

He trails off and the room is silent. I can hear more sobs from Emily

"Oh, for God's sake! What is your problem today? Are you on the rag? I don't need this shit." What a douche. I feel a twinge of sympathy for Emily, but I smash it down. Hard.

She can't stop crying, and he's over it. "Look, I'll go find Leah for you. I can't deal with this. Just..." His voice trails off and I hear the door close.

Voices are coming from the left. "Man, what are you doing in here?" It's Jake. He sounds surprised and disappointed.

"What do you think, stupid? I'm here to see you. I know this is where you hang out. What're ya doing? Waiting to see if your little Venus Fly Trap is going to show up? What a wuss you are. Asking that loser to Homecoming. What a bunch of bullshit, man. The two biggest losers at school showing up at the dance. And with a bunch of other losers as camo. That's worth the price of a ticket, not that I'd ever go to it. I've got better things to do tomorrow night, and they're gonna be a real blast." It's Crazy Cody, sarcastic and hateful.

"Don't call her names, man. Just leave her alone."

"Well, well, well. Aren't you just the knight in shining armor? Rescuing the damsel in distress? Since when do you stick up for anyone but me?"

"Since now. Since I met someone who sees me for myself and isn't just out to use me. That's since when!"

I feel a warm little glow. *He likes me! I knew it!* Jake sounds like he's trying to be tough, but I can hear a little quiver in his voice. So can Cody.

"You pathetic loser!" His voice is full of rage. "You freakin' idiot! How dare you go against me?! You owe me, man, and it's time for you to pay. No one knows about the little Flytrap's locker, do they? Not yet, anyway."

"Man, you know I didn't want to do that."

Jake trashed my locker? It was Jake who put all that nasty stuff in there? How could he do that?

"You think the little Flye will believe you or me when I tell her?"

Then Jake says, "If you tell her that, I'll tell everyone about the dog."

This is a new tone for Jake: strong, firm and really pissed off. I'm proud of him, in spite of the fact I just learned he had something to do with trashing my locker. I think of him helping me pick up the spray cans and muttering, "Sorry." At the time I thought he felt sorry for me; now I think he was apologizing for his own actions.

I hear flesh hitting flesh and Cody yelling, "You fuckin' sonofabitch! You wouldn't dare!"

"Watch me." Jake's voice is frigid and hard. There's no doubt in my mind that he means what he's saying. "Whatever your stupid little scheme is, whatever idiotic thing you have planned, I'm not gonna be a part of it."

I have to do something. I stand up and have my hand on the doorknob when I hear Mr. Lester's voice in the room.

"Stop it right now, boys. What's going on in here?" His voice is cool and level-headed. I can imagine him looking from Jake to Cody, waiting for one of them to speak.

"Nothing, Mr. Lester," Jake mumbles. "Cody and I were just talking about the biology assignment for today. He thinks we're gonna have a test, and I was telling him we're not."

"Is that right? It sounded like you two were getting pretty upset about a little old biology test."

"No, really, Mr. Lester," Cody cuts in, using his smooth, silky voice, and I know he's smiling that creepy little half-grin, looking all meek and humble. "It was just a little misunderstanding. I'm not even supposed to be in here. I just went to the bathroom, saw Jake in here and thought I'd ask him about the test. It's nothing. I've got to get back to Mr. Dickenson before I get in trouble."

His voice changes again, subtly. It's anxious, full of worry. "You won't tell him, will you, Mr. Lester?" He's pleading softly, sounding helpless.

I hear Mr. Lester sigh and then say, "Alright, young man. I'll walk you back to class." The door closes and I hear Jake take a deep, shaky breath.

Chapter Thirty-Nine

I walk home with Jake after school so that we can take more measurements of the tomatoes. The first thing we see is an empty corner where the PVC pipe used to be.

"Mom!" Jake yells into the house and she comes running out, nervously wiping her hands on a towel.

"What?"

"What happened to all that pipe that was in here?"

She sighs in relief and slumps to the threshold of the back door. "Oh my goodness, Jakey, I thought something was wrong. You just gave me another gray hair." She looks at him with loving exasperation.

"Well, where is it?" he persists.

"I don't know. Ask your father. He must have done something with it." She looks at me and says, "Hello, Flye, how are you?"

"I'm fine, ma'am."

"I'll just go get you kids some snacks," she says, closing the door behind her.

Jake and I look at each other and shrug. I don't want to ask any more questions. Jake's dad seems to be a touchy subject.

We turn our attention to the tomatoes. They've grown quite a bit, and we start tying them to some small stakes with strips from old t-shirts that are soft enough that the stems won't break. Some of the leaves are turning yellow, so we pull those off and add fertilizer around the bases. I'm in the process of recording all of our data when Cody's shadow falls across the floor, and I freeze, not wanting to look at Jake, not daring to look at Cody.

"Hey, you guys," Cody says in his normal, soft voice.

"Hey Cody," Jake says, and I turn around, looking first at Jake and then at Cody.

"How's it going, Flye?" Cody looks sane—his eyes are squinting behind his glasses, his hair is not quite as greasy as it usually is, and he's smiling his strange little half-grin. When he's like this he looks so young and vulnerable that I find myself smiling back at him saying, "Hey, Cody, how're you doing?"

"How's the plant experiment going?" We show him the data we've been collecting.

"Cool! This was a great idea you had, Jake." He smiles at both of us, and Jake just looks at him uncomprehendingly. We both know this was Cody's idea, and we both know how quickly his moods can change, so I decide to go while the gettin's good.

I'm walking down the driveway when I hear Cody say to Jake, "Hey, man, I'm sorry I've been giving you so much shit about Flye. You're right about her; she is nice, and I'm glad y'all

182

are going to Homecoming together." I stop dead in my tracks, but I don't dare turn around. What?! Is there a third person inside Cody? I'm more afraid of this nice Cody, the Cody who can tuck away all his sickness and his hatred, than the crazy one. At least I can see that Cody coming; this one is unpredictable.

When I get home, I hack into Cody's laptop and can't believe what I see. Everything's been wiped clean, including his folders on his desktop, the Ninja background, and his screensaver. His browser history has nothing on it, not even an email to Jake.

What's he up to? This is not the Cody I know and fear. It's like he's trying to wipe out his entire history, his entire existence.

Chapter Forty

It's Homecoming Day. And it's my first Cameo lunch. Toni glides across the floor as Dexter and Lily walk in. I say hey to all of them and we sit at a long table and start pulling out our lunches. I have a couple of pieces of veggie pizza and an apple; Georgia pulls out sushi from the local health food store; and Dexter is munching on carrot and celery sticks. Lily looks at him and then at his lunch with a slight frown and he says, "Really, darlin', do you have to ask? I'm the biggest thing around here since four hundred pounds of sliced bread."

The Meerkat comes back after heating up some soup and we all start talking about the magazine.

"We've got quite a few submissions already," Lily starts.

"Are they any good?" Camille wants to know. Toni starts scrolling through them on her laptop.

"Not bad to start with anyway. There are some nice black and white photos and some poetry that needs a little work;

there's also a short story that's, well..." Lily trails off, not knowing how to say "it sucks" politely.

"We may need to send it back?" Georgia finishes for her.

"Yeah. Definitely."

We continue to look over the submissions, culling ones we can't use and making notes about others. Toni says, "Flye, I hear you're a genius with publishing software. Do you think you could help me after school with formatting some of these new submissions?"

"Well, I don't know about the 'genius' part but sure, I'd love to."

After school, Jenn, Katie, and Taylor stop by my locker. "Let's all meet at the game at five and then after we go home to change, Katie and I'll pick everyone up so that we can go to the dance together." Jenn is definitely on top of this.

"Wanna walk home with us, Flye?" Katie and Taylor say in unison.

"Nah, I've still got a couple of things to do for *Cameo*. I'll see you at the game, 'K?"

As soon as the building looks empty, I'm in the Box. I just need a little time and space before I jump into this new social life I have that seems to be great but is a little scary too; it's so unfamiliar.

Yeah, right. What a good justifier you are. You're going through withdrawals; you can't stop thinking about it when you're not in here. You need to start looking into Eavesdroppers Anonymous.

I hear a voice coming from the cafeteria. The cheerleaders are probably still in there, finishing up the decorations for the dance.

"—pack the fertilizer in real tight—"

"It is tight!"

"No, pack it together. It has to explode evenly."

I stop breathing and my heart pounds in my head. It's Cody, whispering in his cold, insane voice. I'm sick in my stomach and my head is full of everything I've read about Columbine and Eric Harris and Dylan Klebold. I remember how Eric Harris's penname was RebDoomer and Cody's penname is RebDoomerII; I remember the poetry about death and darkness and dying signed by the same name; I remember his screen saver dripping the bloody words, "Four twenty forever." I remember the PVC pipe that mysteriously appeared and then disappeared from Jake's garage and all the fertilizer we bought. I can hear Cody telling Jake just yesterday how Homecoming will be a blast. I remember his slithering voice whispering, *"We'll be famous..."* I start to shake as it finally all comes together.

Cody's in the cafeteria making bombs to blow up the school. I have to do something right now!

"No, no, no!" It's Little Cody, whimpering and scared. "I don't want to do this! I can't! I'll get in so much trouble!"

"You fuckin' pansy ass! You can't wimp out on me now! Cody..." the voice is more chilling than I've ever heard him sound. "You have to do what Eric tells you. You always do what Eric tells you! NOW DO IT!!!"

Cody is sobbing, gasping for air. I can hear something hard clunk on the cafeteria floor and the sound of a plastic bag being dragged and I scream, holding my head and shaking, in the confines of my Box.

"Help me! Somebody! Help me!" No one can hear me. No one can help me.

I curl up in the fetal position on the floor, trembling, tears running down my face, waiting for everything to go black. Images pour into my mind: Mom and Dad and Stoner and me laughing at the dinner table; Bekkah and me at the park, swinging so high into the sky it felt like we were in orbit, that we'd never come down. And things that will never happen now: my first date with Jake; my first kiss; high school graduation. I whimper with terror and grief for my life that I'll never live. It isn't supposed to end this way.

"Put the wire in. DO IT NOW!" Eric roars.

The walls of the Box begin to glow faintly in purple and red and orange, like I've stared directly at a sunset and then looked away. The colors fill my mind and my body and my heart and I go catapulting out of the Box, up the stairs, and down the hall toward the cafeteria.

Chapter Forty-One

It's dim in here, covered in streamers and tiny colored lights, with a glittery disco ball in the center of the ceiling. The cheerleaders have been in here all afternoon decorating for the dance and it looks like a movie set, until I see Cody standing off to the side with a pile of white pipes, duct taped together. He's wearing a white jacket and I can see his cell phone in his hand. He's looking around like he's lost. I can hear him talking to himself.

"Eric keeps telling me to put fertilizer in these pipes... they'll protect me from the shadows...they want to kill me..." It's Little Cody and he's looking around in panic.

I start to walk towards him, but I can't move my legs. I don't know what to do.

"Cody!" I try to speak clearly and calmly, but it comes out in a whisper and he doesn't seem to know I'm here.

"Cody!" This time he hears me.

"What the fuck do you want, you fucking little flytrap?"

"Cody, don't..."

"Oh, Cody...don't hurt the wittle Fwye Twap...she's too good for us...thinks she knows everything. Get the hell outta here, you fuckin' bitch!" Eric is mocking, raging, and coming towards me.

His face changes instantly, becoming the softer, scared face of Cody. He holds out the pipe to me and I instinctively recoil.

"I can't do this alone."

"You don't have to Cody. I'm here. I can help you. Why don't you come with me?" Finally I've found my voice. I take a deep breath, trying to calm myself down. All I can think about is getting us both out of here.

"Jake was supposed to help me but he won't, the rat bastard. He's not my friend. He's never been my friend. He's a bloodsucker. He just wants my power." I thought he was talking to me, but he's not. He's talking to someone I can't see, listening to someone I can't hear, as he keeps walking towards me.

Oh God. What I thought was a white jacket is a series of pipe bombs, all taped together and strung around his body. I can see wires sticking out of them and he fidgets with his cell phone and I lose my breath, shaking so violently I can barely stand up. His cell phone is the detonator.

"I'm so scared."

"You can trust me, Cody." I keep my voice calm and reassuring, even though all I want to do is scream and run, and I start walking toward him.

"Stay back, you dumb bitch!" Eric is screaming at me with Cody's twisted, raging face.

"Eric, tell Cody to stop." I try to sound authoritative but it comes out quivering and breathless, and Eric laughs, a blood-chilling cackle.

"Oh, the wittle Fwye Twap wants Cody to stop, does she?"

"Please, Cody, if you can hear me, please stop, please don't do this—"

I gather all the strength I have and keep walking. Almost there.

"Just trust me, Cody." Tears are running down my face and I can hardly breathe. *I don't know what to do here; I'm just a kid. What if I make him even madder? What if I just make things worse? Where's Mr. Lester? Isn't there anyone else here in this godforsaken place?*

"Help! Somebody help! Help me!" I'm screaming at the top of my lungs, making myself hoarse, screaming so loudly I think I'm going to throw up.

Eric laughs. "You stupid bitch, there's no one here. Why do you think we picked this time? Did you think we'd do it in the middle of the pep rally?"

"Cody, please, don't do this. Let's just get out of here. You don't have to do this—"

"Don't trust her, you idiot! She hates you!"

"Is she a shadow?"

"I'm real, Cody, and I don't hate you. I like you. I'd like to be friends with you."

"You fuckin' idiot, don't believe her, she hates us. She wants to kill us!"

"Eric, I don't want to kill you. I don't want anyone to die. Not you. Not Cody. Not me." I'm sobbing so hard I don't know if he can understand me. I reach out my hand and Cody fidgets with his cell phone, turning it around and around.

"DO IT NOW! PUSH THE FUCKING BUTTON! RIGHT! NOW!"

"CODY, DON'T!" I'm sobbing and shaking, begging for my life. "Eric, please let him go. Don't make him do this. I know you don't want to do this. Not really."

"WHAT THE HELL DO YOU KNOW ABOUT ME?! YOU DON'T KNOW ANYTHING!"

Eric is in complete control now, and his finger hovers over the send button. I'm on the edge of passing out as the room goes black, like in a movie scene with just Cody and me in a spotlight and I can see my life clearly, how I've always thought that there's just one right answer, one key to every door that will make me popular and happy and always knowing what to do. What a load of crap. The only answer is me; the only key is me, who I am right now, my own self and what I choose to do with my life. That's the only thing I can control.

I look at Cody and I can see him as if he's bathed in sunlight, a little boy before the demons came to visit and decided to stay. His young face is smiling with joy and innocence; the haunted fear on his face is gone. This is who he really is, without this sickness or whatever it is controlling him. We gaze at each other for a long moment and then it ends and the spotlight is gone and it's just Cody and Eric and me in the cafeteria surrounded by weapons of mass destruction and our lives are literally in Eric's hands.

I can't afford to be scared anymore. I take another deep breath, forcing myself to be calm, forcing myself to be the grownup here, even though I'm not.

"C'mon, Cody, just give me the cell phone." I step closer to him, holding out my hand and he jerks away, his finger on the send key, looking desperately around at what only he can see.

"Press the button! DO IT NOW!" His finger is on the button.

"No, I can't. It's a bad thing. I'll get in trouble…"

"Cody, give me the cell phone."

"DON'T GIVE IT TO HER! PRESS THE FUCKING BUTTON!"

Cody's finger is on the button and there's no more time. There will be no more time, no more space, no more anything, ever. I'm beyond thinking. What happens next will happen. All I've got is right now.

I lunge at the phone, feeling its hard plastic brush against my hand as I stumble and fall to my knees. The phone flips off the tips of my fingers and hits the floor with a bang that echoes in the quiet cafeteria, and for a split second I think the bombs have exploded. Evidently Cody thinks so too, because he's down on his knees, his head bent toward the floor with his hands around his head. The phone skids across the hard, linoleum floor and stops, wedged under a table leg off to the side and parallel to the rest of the bombs.

You know how people say in times of crisis like this, everything slows down? That's not true. Everything speeds up. Cody's pale, cringing face immediately morphs into a mask of rage and hatred, his mouth a screaming cavern and we both run, skidding and slipping, toward the phone. He's ahead of me, outdistancing me, and I slide on my belly, diving for his legs, grabbing him and pulling him down to the floor as we both careen under the table and my head makes solid contact with the table's pedestal but I don't feel a thing. The phone is stuck tightly and Cody is on top of me, clawing maniacally at me, the table, the floor, thin air, anything he can get to, trying desperately to get to the phone before I do.

Oh God, what if the jostling of the table accidentally hits the send button? What if Cody gets it before I do? A superhuman strength, borne of fear and adrenaline, envelopes me and I rear up and back, hitting the table again, with Cody still on my back and spin both of us around, as I pin him to the floor.

"DAMN YOU, ERIC! GET OUT OF HERE AND LEAVE HIM ALONE!" My voice rings with a strength and confidence that I don't recognize. I have no idea where this is coming from. "I MEAN IT! HE DOESN'T NEED YOU! GET AWAY FROM US!"

Cody's face goes soft again and he starts to cry. "Flye? I didn't mean it." He's Cody again. I don't know how long he'll stay here, but it's long enough. I grab the phone.

Chapter Forty-Two

The plastic is cold in my hand. There's no explosion. No flames. No death. Icy relief washes over me as I try to stay calm, ignoring the violent shaking that envelopes me and threatens to bring me to my knees. I shove the phone deep in my pocket while pulling out my own cell phone and dial 9-1-1 for the second time in a week.

All is silent except for the sound of Cody's and my breathing. I gulp in air, trying to process the fact that we're both still alive. I sit down, putting my head between my legs, feeling the blood rushing to my head and am suddenly aware of Cody sitting next to me. I glance at him sideways, not wanting to startle him. He's just sitting there, his pale hair falling over his dead-white face, his colorless eyes staring at nothing. He seems harmless right now, but I know how quickly he can change—how Eric can emerge with lightning speed.

I don't know what to do for him. I am so out of my league here. I look at him more directly and a wave of pity washes over me. Whatever's going on with him, I'm certain he's not doing any of this on purpose and I get why Jake hangs with him, takes care of him, and looks after him. It's easy to feel sorry for Cody.

"9-1-1. What is your emergency?" The voice echoes in the silence and I jump, almost dropping my phone.

"There's a bomb at New Hope High. I mean, someone tried to bomb it. I mean, there's a bunch of bombs here. Oh, God, please help me!" My voice trails off on an inhuman wail as the enormity of the situation hits me again and again and again. The relief of having someone who actually knows what they're doing on the other end of the phone is overwhelming and all I can do is sob, "Please come. He's still here. There're bombs everywhere."

"I'm dispatching help right now." The voice is calm, reassuring and, most importantly, adult. For the first time since this whole nightmare started, I have a glimmer of hope that we might not die after all.

"Stay on the line, Miss. I'm going to ask you some questions and I want you to try to answer them for me as best you can. Do you understand?"

The voice is so soft, her lilting Southern accent so normal, so sane, so real, that all I can do is nod my head.

"Miss? Are you still there?"

"Yes," I manage to cough out. "I'm still here."

"And what is your name, dear?"

I tell her, and she wants to know if anyone else is with me.

"Cody McDaniel. He's a student here. We're both students here."

"You said that the bomber was still there. Where is he or she?"

I look at the phone in disbelief. Seriously? But then I realize that she can't possibly know what's been happening here. "It's Cody. He's sitting next to me wearing a bunch of pipe bombs. I have the detonator."

"Stay calm."

Yeah right, do you think you could do that?

"Under no circumstances are you to touch the bombs or try in any way to disarm them. Now move to a safe distance away from the perpetrator."

What? Like I'm going to do that? The only way to keep Cody calm is to stay here with him. Besides, he can't do anything without the detonator. I touch the phone, deep in my jeans pocket, to make sure it's still there. Looking at Cody again, he's still calm; in fact, he looks sleepy, like he's exhausted. He probably is. I know I am.

"Okay, I'm away from him," I lie.

"Help is on the way," the reassuring voice continues. "Are you injured?"

"Well, I hit my head on the table, but I'm okay. I'm not bleeding or anything..."

"Is the perpetrator injured?"

"His name is Cody, and no, he doesn't seem to be injured..."
His injuries aren't the kind you can see.

"Tell me everything you can remember."

"I came into the cafeteria after school and found Cody with pipe bombs..."

She asks a few questions here and there and I can hear her keyboard clicking as she takes notes. "...and then I got the detonator away from him and I called you."

"You're a very brave girl. Help is on the way. I want you to stay on the line with me until they get there. Do you understand?" The voice is lulling me into a feeling of safety. How can she do that, when Cody's right here wrapped in bombs and I can feel the detonator pressing into my hip? I laugh out loud and the sound makes me jump, as if someone else is laughing.

"Are you alright, Flye?" The voice sounds alarmed and it's my turn to reassure her.

"Yeah, I guess so. I mean, this is all so crazy. I'm just feeling a little insane here, is all."

"You and me both." It's Cody speaking and I look at him, startled and suddenly afraid again. He's staring at me with that little half grin of his and he still looks okay, but you never know. Is Eric coming out?

I venture a tentative question. "Hey, Cody. How're you feeling?"

He laughs, not a crazy Eric laugh but a sad, hopeless little sound. "I'm still here."

"Is Eric here, too?" I have to ask, even though I'm afraid anything I say or do may incite Eric's wrath and he'll be back. So far it appears that only Cody is here.

"Flye, I hear voices. Are you alright?" The operator sounds alarmed.

"Yeah, I'm fine. I'm just talking to the perp—to Cody."

"You should avoid all contact with him if at all possible."

197

"Well, I've found that this helps keep him calm."

Cody is looking at me in amazement and snorts derisively but his hair is back from his face and I can see his eyes, peaceful, but sad and hopeless. "For someone who's supposed to be so smart, you really can be kinda dumb, cantcha?"

I just shrug, not knowing what he's talking about, and look at him, waiting for signs of sudden rage, preparing to do battle all over again.

He sighs and looks at me like I'm a not-very-smart kindergartner. "Eric is always with me, Flye. He lives in here." He's taps his head and then shakes it in frustration.

"I've been like this for a couple of years now. No one knows, not even Jake. I've tried really hard to hide it—to hide him. But he's getting stronger. Or maybe I'm getting weaker."

He sighs and all I want to do is hug him but I can't touch the bombs. I inch my hand over to his and lay it next to his cold, scrawny hand. He looks down and smiles but doesn't move. Neither do I.

"Do you know what it's like living two separate lives and hearing voices from people you can't see?"

I think of the Box. The time I spent in there was exactly like what Cody's describing. Well, maybe not exactly, but close enough.

"I think I can imagine it," I say, still watching him carefully, looking for signs of Eric.

He scoffs again. "No, you can't. You're lucky. You have no idea what I'm talking about."

"I think I get you better than you know, Cody." I start to say and then we're interrupted by the sound of sirens approaching. Cody jumps up fearfully and I stand up next to him.

"It's okay. It's just the ambulance, and someone who's going to take these pipes off you." I try to be reassuring but he's starting to panic again and I'm waiting for Eric to show up any second now.

"It's okay. It's okay. It's okay." I keep whispering it to him like a mantra, trying to keep him calm, trying to make him feel safe, trying to keep Eric at bay. Police cars and an ambulance pull up out front, cut the siren and two policemen walk into the building.

"We're in here—straight ahead," I call.

The SWAT team walks quickly, but calmly, into the cafeteria. One of them turns to me and asks, "Are you the girl who has the detonator?"

I nod and take Cody's phone out of my pocket, handing it to him. He takes it outside, where I see him give it to other SWAT team members, who begin to disarm it. More SWAT team guys walk inside in military formation toward Cody, as one of them escorts me outside.

Cody calls out to me. "Flye, don't go! Don't leave!"

I can see panic fluttering on his face, and I know that Eric is hovering around his consciousness, ready to appear right now. "You've gotta keep him calm," I say to the cop who has my arm. He doesn't say anything. I scream at him, "Eric's coming out!"

One of the SWAT guys by Cody motions to an EMT who's hovering outside by the front door. The EMT sprints inside towards Cody.

"Hey, buddy, looks like you need a little help here." The EMT swabs Cody's left arm with alcohol and gets ready to inject a needle.

"Flye? Flye! They're gonna kill me! Don't let them kill me, Flye!" Cody is panicking, trying to get away from the firm grip both cops have on his arms.

"It's okay, Cody. We're not trying to kill you." The EMT soothes him down and Cody relaxes for just an instant. I see the EMT plunge the needle into the soft flesh of his arm as the cop guides me outside past the crime scene tape surrounding the school. Another SWAT team with dogs enters the building with the same military-like precision.

A woman EMT rolls a stretcher inside, and a few minutes later they roll it out again with Cody on it. The bombs have been removed from his body, his eyes are half-shut, and his arms and legs are firmly bound to the sides of the stretcher. One of the EMTs shields Cody's eyes against the bright sunlight and it's like I'm just now realizing that it's still daylight. It feels like it should be midnight. Cody is starting to doze off as they lift the stretcher carefully into the back of the ambulance and I watch from my safe distance behind the tape.

His eyes catch mine for a brief moment and I can barely hear him, but I think he whispers, "I didn't mean it. I wouldn't have done it. I'm sorry."

I sink into the warmth of the soft green grass next to the sidewalk as the ambulance pulls away, lights flashing, siren silenced. Images flash through my mind: Cody wrapped up in pipes, his face changing every second as he, Little Cody and Eric battled inside his mind; the detonator skidding across the floor and Cody and me scratching and scrambling for it. My head is aching where I slammed it against the table. *It's over. It's over. It's over.* I feel like I'm a thousand years old, like I've lived ten lifetimes in the last hour.

It's not over for Cody. I hope he'll be okay. I have to believe that he'll be okay, because if he isn't, then what's the point of anything? Poor Cody.

A small movement from off to my right distracts me and I turn, fearful again. *Eric? No, it can't be. Eric is on his way to the hospital. Eric and Cody and Little Cody and everyone else inside Cody's head.*

Mr. Lester stands there, watching me carefully. Our eyes meet and he smiles quietly, nodding, and tipping his cap.

Chapter Forty-Three

"Flye? FLYE!" Mom screams at me, running up to me and enveloping me in a hug, enfolding me, protecting me. I look up and see Dad right beside her, grabbing us both. Behind them, Jenn, Evan, Taylor, Katie, and Jake are running to me.

"Mom! What are you doing here?" I can't believe they're all here. "How did you know?"

"The police called me at work and I went and got Dad and we came right away. And then we saw Jenn and everyone."

"I was getting worried about you when you didn't show up, so we came back over here. We met the ambulance on its way out," Jenn says excitedly.

Everyone starts talking all at once.

"Are you okay?"

"Oh my God, what happened—?"

"We heard there were bombs—"

"Who did this—?"

I take a deep breath. I so don't want to rat Cody out, but I don't know what else to do. "It was Cody," I begin, and proceed to tell them the whole story. "And the police came and the ambulance took him away—"

Jake interrupts me. "Flye, is Cody okay?" His eyes are huge with fear and welling with unshed tears. I feel so bad for him; this is his best friend, the kid he grew up with.

I hug him unashamedly. "He's on his way to the hospital. He's gonna be okay." I hope I'm telling him the truth.

The tears start to flow down his cheeks and he does nothing to stop them. "I should've known. I should've done something. He was always dropping these hints and I just didn't listen. I didn't get it. I didn't want to get it."

I'm still holding him, whispering in his ear. "It's not your fault. There was nothing you could have done. You didn't know how sick he was. No one knew."

Except me. I knew something was up and I refused to see it. I didn't want to lose my precious Box, my precious so-called status, my precious so-called power. This is all my fault. I could've stopped it and I didn't.

A car pulls up at the cub and Jake's mom hurtles towards us. "Jake! Jake! Are you all right?" She grabs Jake in a tight hug and he clings to her, tears falling.

"Mom?"

"It's okay, Jakey, everything's going to be okay."

She looks at the rest of us over Jake's shoulder. "It's all over the radio. Someone had bombs?" Her voice rises in disbelief.

"It was Cody, Mom." Jake's voice is low and full of pain.

"Cody?! No. It can't be. Cody would never do something like this. Flye?" She looks at me like I have all the answers and I don't even know the questions.

"Yes, ma'am, it was him." I start to tell the story yet again.

When I finish, she turns back to Jake. "Did he say anything to you? Did you know anything about this?"

She keeps holding him close, rocking him back and forth, like he's a baby and I realize that he is. He's her baby and it's just now hitting her that she could've lost him. She just keeps rocking him.

"His poor parents," she murmurs. "This will just kill them. It's killing me. He's like a second son to me. He was just at our house last night for supper. He was fine. How can this be? I've known him since he was a baby. He's the nicest, sweetest kid— the last person you'd ever think of to do something like this."

"I don't know, Mom. I guess I should've known. I should've done something."

"How could you have known? I didn't know. You couldn't have done anything."

I walk over to them and Jake's mom puts an arm around me, dabbing uselessly at the tears rolling down her face. "I'm just so glad you kids are alright. And Flye, you're a hero. You're amazing. What you went through in there—what you did for him—for all of us," she gestures toward the school, "I could never have done that, not in a million years."

We stand around outside, huddled in our fear and sorrow and total misery when suddenly, Mr. Lester is standing next to us.

"Little Flye Girl," he says, "there's a detective here who needs to talk with you."

Jake and his mom huddle with my mom and our friends as Dad goes with me and we walk over to a tall, dark-haired man in a suit. I look behind me and see more cops going to meet Mr. Brauer, who has just pulled up and is getting out of his car.

The detective looks at me closely. "Miss Shannahan? We'd like you to answer some questions, please, if you don't mind."

My dad jumps in immediately. "Flye is a minor, Detective. You may question her in my presence, but if I feel we need a lawyer present, you will have to wait until our attorney arrives."

"Of course, Mr. Shannahan." The detective is respectful and soft-spoken and I realize he's just doing his job.

But oh my God. I need a lawyer? Am I in trouble? Do they think I helped Cody? The detective asks me to tell what happened, so I begin.

"I was staying late after school, helping with our school's literary magazine and I heard sounds from the cafeteria..."

I go on to tell them about seeing Cody in the cafeteria with all the pipe bombs, how he was talking to Eric and how he almost set off the bombs. "And then I called 9-1-1."

I don't want Cody to be in trouble with the law so I add, "I think he was hallucinating or something. He was acting crazy or something—like he wasn't himself."

The officer looks at me with a keen stare. "Did Cody at any time ask you for your help?"

What?! "No," I say, staring him right in the eye.

"He didn't try to get you to assist him in any way?" *I knew it. I am a suspect. He thinks I'm an accomplice.*

Again, I look straight at him and say with all the conviction I can muster, "No. Absolutely not."

"And you had no idea what he was planning?"

Oh crap. How do I answer this? Yeah, I knew he was planning something, but I had no idea it would be this bad. I had no idea it would be this specific thing—an attempted bombing. Still, I should have gone to Mr. Lester any one of those times that I had decided to and then chickened out at the last minute. Maybe I am an accomplice after all.

The silence is growing and both Dad and the cop are looking at me intently. I sigh, close my eyes and shake my head. *No. I didn't know he was planning on bombing the school.* The officer continues to study me intently, looks at Dad and then back to me.

"You did a very brave thing, young lady," the officer smiles at me kindly and then looks at my dad. "Those are all the questions we have for now, but if anything else comes up, we'll be in touch."

Jenn comes racing up to me before he can say another word. "Mr. Brauer just cancelled the game and the dance. The police are still searching the building for more bombs."

Press cars from local TV stations pull up and start grabbing microphones and cameras. Now that any immediate danger is over, my friends are acting all hyper, like they're in a TV crime show. Nothing this big has ever happened at NHH. Reporters are milling through the crowd, trying to interview the detective and anyone else who looks like they might know something.

Only Jake and I are quiet, standing off to the side in the shade, watching and clinging to each other like orphans in a foreign country, just holding each other and trembling.

I whisper, "It's okay."

"No, it's not."

"It'll be okay."

"I should've known."

"I know, me too."

"How could you have known? You barely knew Cody." Jake draws back and looks at me, puzzled and confused.

"Yeah, well, I dunno, I just should have...what's the use in having people think I'm so smart if I can't do something good with it?" I stammer and blush, ashamed and alarmed at having almost given myself away.

He smiles at me through his tears, pulls my head down to his shoulder and cradles me there. I smell his warm skin, a hint of aftershave and the salt of his sweat, all mixed together and I feel safer than I have since coming to this school. He murmurs, "You *are* smart. And you *did* do something good."

Jenn and the others come bounding over to us, still high on excitement but stop abruptly when they see Jake and me still crying. Jenn hugs me from the back and then they're all over us, holding us both in a group hug, murmuring, comforting, reassuring.

"It's okay—"

"You were so brave—"

"It's gonna be okay—"

"We'll take care of you—"

"Cody's gonna be okay—"

Jenn hands me a tissue and a candy bar. I laugh through my tears as she grins apologetically. "Well, chocolate always works for me."

Dad walks over to me. "Flye, the reporters want to ask you some questions. I can do that for you, if you want. You've already been through so much, and you're a minor."

I wipe my eyes and blow my nose, disentangling myself from the group. "No, it's fine."

He looks at me worriedly and starts to protest. I put my hand on his sleeve and look him straight in the eye.

"Dad. It's okay. I've got this."

I glance back at Jake, who's still surrounded by the rest of our friends. He gives me a shaky smile and a "thumbs up." I smile back, take a deep breath, stand up straight, square my shoulders, and walk over to face the crowd.

Chapter Forty-Four

The weekend passes in a haze of TV reports, post-traumatic stress nightmares and time spent alone with Stoner, who raced home as soon as he heard the news.

It's finally Monday—back to school. Mom parks in front of the school and goes in to sign Jake and me out as we wait in the backseat of her car. Pulling away from the curb, she heads toward Chapel Hill and says, "I checked with his doctors. He's expecting you."

We ride the rest of the way in silence, broken only by the radio with its incessant news about Cody and the bombs. "Young Flye Shannahan is a local hero, detaining a potential bomber at New Hope High on Friday just prior to the school's Homecoming. The suspect has been taken into custody." Jake and I glance at each other and grimace; we've been hearing this crap all weekend and I, for one, am totally sick to death of it.

"Mom, could you just turn the radio off, please?"

She pushes the button and we ride the rest of the way in total silence.

Mom pulls up in front of University Hospital and leads us up to the adolescent psychiatric floor. At the desk, she says, "This is Flye Shannahan and Jake Christianson. We're here to visit Cody McDaniel."

The nurse asks us to leave all jewelry, pens, belts and any other items that could potentially be used as a weapon and then escorts us down a long hall to Cody's room. It's not as bad as I thought it would be, but the doors all have wire mesh imbedded in the glass windows and an armed guard is sitting outside the room we stop at. I look at Mom like, *"What the...?"* and she whispers, "He's under arrest, and he's also on suicide watch."

Mom waits in the hall as the guard escorts us into the room, stands against the door with his arms folded across his chest, and tells us we have ten minutes. The room is small, narrow and completely without any adornment on the institutional brown walls. I notice that the bathroom door is locked, and looking at the guard, he says laconically, "To keep him from hurting himself."

Cody is lying in a hospital bed, with the side railings up. He's dressed in gray sweat pants and a green and gold NHH hoodie without the drawstring. His head is swathed in the hood so that I can barely see his face, but his eyes are open. I can see them gleaming palely in the filtered sunlight coming through his window, which is nailed shut and has bars on it. He smiles when he sees us, says, "Hey, Flye," and low fives with Jake, since his wrists are fastened to the sides of the bed.

"Welcome to the funny farm." He looks at Jake and says, "I really screwed up big time, didn't I, man?"

"Yeah, well, it could've been a lot worse." Jake tries to smile and blow off the fact that Cody's locked up in a psych ward, but his face crumbles and tears roll down his cheeks.

"Hey, man, it's okay. It's all good. I'll be getting outta here any day now and then I'm really gonna kick your ass at chess."

Now it's my turn to get teary. If Cody goes anywhere at all, it'll be to a courtroom and maybe a prison cell.

"So what's it like in here?" Jake is searching, trying to make some kind of small talk but neither one of us is what you'd call experienced in carrying on a conversation in a locked room with an armed guard present.

"Oh, you know, the usual, golf, tennis, swimming, hot chicks. It's a fuckin' country club." Cody laughs a little. He seems fairly normal, at least compared to how I last saw him, and he's trying to put up a brave front but it's not working. He looks so little and scared and alone, I just want to rush to him and hug him. He starts talking again, but he's pretty much just rambling.

"Yeah, some crazy times, huh? Hey, what's the name of that dude that used to play online chess with us—can't remember his name, man."

"It was ZoomBro," Jake fills in for him, but I don't think Cody's listening.

"Hey, man, remember kindergarten?"

Jake smiles. "Yeah, I remember parts of it. What about it?"

"Remember when we decided to quit school because we weren't in the same class?"

Jake laughs. "Yeah. And your mom called my mom and said that she had us in her car. She'd found us walking the railroad tracks into town." He trails off, remembering a simpler time when both he and Cody were little kids together.

Cody laughs too. "Oh my God, we were in so much trouble!"

Probably nothing compared to now, though.

"Yeah, and remember when we camped out that time in your backyard, and it started to rain, and the tent was leaking, and I just wanted to go home but you wouldn't let me, so we stuck it out, and our sleeping bags were practically floating in the morning?"

"Yeah, man, but we did it. How old were we?"

"I dunno, maybe second grade?"

"Oh God, remember the time we were gonna get summer jobs picking strawberries at the farm down the road from us, and we showed up the first day, but they had new baby kittens in the barn, and all we wanted to do was play with the kittens?"

"Yeah, we got fired after the first hour."

They keep talking and laughing about all the life they've shared together, and they seem more like brothers than just friends. This is a side of both of them that I've never seen before—young, carefree, with an aura of innocence still lingering on their laughing faces, and I can't stop myself from crying and grieving everything they've lost. Everything we've all lost.

"So how was Homecoming?" Cody's fading out of lucidity as he comes back to the present. His eyes drift around the room and then close momentarily.

"They cancelled it, because of, you know..." Jake trails off, embarrassed.

"But it's okay, Cody, they're going to have it later..." I trail off too. I don't know what to say to him.

He looks at me again and says, "Hey, Flye, how ya doin'?"

"I'm fine, Cody, I've been here all along."

"How're the tomato plants doing?" He closes his eyes again, and I think he's sleeping, but then he jerks back to the present and starts running his hands over the bed sheet. He's agitated, and starts talking faster.

"Yeah, they're running all these tests on me but what they're really doing is scanning my brain."

"They're not scanning your brain, Cody." Jake tries to be reassuring but he looks at me uncertainly. "Maybe they were like, doing an MRI or something?"

I just shrug and say, "The tomatoes are doing great. They're growing really fast, with all the fert—" Oh God, I can't say anything without sticking my foot in my mouth.

But he doesn't seem to hear me, he's gazing off into space, and then says, "Yeah, they're drawing my blood and checking it for signs of contamination, you know, in case they did something bad to me."

"No one's doing anything bad to you, Cody."

"Shhh!" Cody glances around the room, motioning to the cop with his head.

There's a knock at the door and a nurse with cartoon figures on her slacks and smock enters with a syringe, which she injects efficiently into Cody's left arm.

"Thank you, Nurse Ratchett," he murmurs and I clamp my hand over my mouth as I involuntarily grin. I glance at Jake to see if he gets it, but he's watching Cody drift off on a sedated buzz. The guard tells us it's time to leave, and I turn to walk out the door, glancing back at Cody one last time.

His eyes flash open, clear, lucid, and sweet. "Thanks, Flye, you know, for saving my life."

We walk out into the hall where Mom is waiting, and I collapse in tears. Jake is standing there with tears streaming down his face, trying not to let me see him cry, and Mom puts her arms around both of us, drawing us into a safe, protective circle. We just stand there for a long time, not believing how sick Cody is and how real this all is.

Finally, I say, "It's not supposed to be like this. He should just be a, you know, a normal kid, maybe with some problems, yeah, but not this." I trail off, trying to understand something I can't possibly understand, something I never will understand, even if I live a thousand years.

And Jake says again, "I should've known. I should've done something."

I look at him, looking so lost and realize that he truly is lost. He's lost his best friend and his sort-of-brother, but even more than that, he's lost all his dreams for the future he always imagined that would have Cody in it. Who will his future hold now?

Mom gives us both a squeeze and says, "There's Cody's mom. I'm going to go talk to her. Do you kids just want to wait here or come along or what?"

Jake looks guiltily at Cody's mom, standing by the nurse's station, and then back at me and it's easy to see that he's dreading talking to her because he didn't take care of her son like he's always done.

"We'll be there in a minute," I tell her and put my arm around Jake. I search for the right words to say. Nothing in my life has prepared me for this and I feel so helpless.

"It was cool listening to you and Cody talk about stuff you guys used to do," I begin, floundering for words of wisdom. "You guys are so close. Kinda like me and Bekkah. Like we just know each other's thoughts without having to say anything." *Oh, God, what good is this doing? All I'm talking about is myself and this is not about me.*

"Yeah, I can't remember a time when Cody wasn't in my life, when we weren't doing stuff together. I just don't know…"

He doesn't know how he's going to live his life without Cody. I mean, it's not like Cody is dead, but it sort of is, because everything will be so different now. I look at Jake's face, full of loss and sorrow and see the deep grief carved there. I don't think Jake will ever be the same again. I know I won't.

I try again. "You've got me. And Jenn and Katie and Taylor and Evan…" I begin.

He looks at me curiously with the beginnings of hope filtering through. "Do I have you?"

He's looking at me so intensely that I blush bright red and can't meet his eyes. *Get a grip, Flye. After everything you've just been through, stop acting like a little kid with her first crush.*

But I am a little kid with my first crush.

Yeah, yeah, whatever. Get over it.

I look straight into Jakes eyes and say, "You've got me for a friend...for as long as...whatever..."

"Just a friend?"

All I want to do is blush more, giggle helplessly, and run home to IM with Bekkah. But that's ridiculous now. Those days are gone. I say, "No, not just a friend."

He smiles at me through his tears, the first real, genuine smile I've seen on his face since Friday before Cody, before our world tilted, before we grew up. Maybe too fast. Maybe too soon. But we did grow up.

We walk over to Mom and hear Cody's mom saying, "We had no idea. He's always seemed so normal to us—our sweet boy. He'd never do something like this. And now the press is blaming us."

At this she dissolves in tears and Mom puts her arms around her. It's like a funeral around here, everyone crying and mourning. But really, it's worse. Cody's still alive, still so sick, and no one knows what's going to happen to him.

Jake goes to Mrs. McDaniel and puts his arm around her. "Oh, Jakey! I'm so glad you came to see him. How is he?" And again I'm struck by how close Jake is to Cody's family, how Cody's mom is treating Jake like another son, how this is a McDaniel-Christianson family tragedy, and how glad I am that Mrs. McDaniel has Jake to comfort her. No matter what happens.

She turns to me. "Flye, I'm so sorry. So sorry you had to be there when it happened. But I'm so grateful that you were. You saved my boy. How can I ever thank you?"

I flush again, embarrassed by this adult I barely know being so humble towards me.

"Uh, it's okay, I just happened to be there and, uh, I just did what I thought I should..." I trail off, not knowing what else to say. This seems so lame, so I try again. "I mean, I'm glad he's okay, that he's going to be okay. I'm glad he's getting some help." Oh, God, that's even worse. "I'm just glad we got to see him," I finish in a rush.

She smiles at me, chin quivering, mouth uncertain and gives me a hug. "Bless your heart, sweetie. You come with Jake to see him anytime you want."

She thanks all of us again, gives a little wave and then turns, straightens her back, lifts her chin, and walks with calm purpose down the hall to Cody's room.

We get in the car and drive away. "Mom, do you think Cody's going to be okay?" Jake and I exchange glances, and then Mom's and my eyes meet in the rearview mirror. *Don't treat me like a kid 'cause I'm not. Don't give me some bubble gum and cotton candy bullshit. Tell me the truth.*

Mom blows her nose with one hand while driving with the other and drops her gaze back to the road. There's a long silence.

"Cody's a sick boy, but I believe he'll be able to get better. Once they get a diagnosis, and figure out how to help him, he could lead a fairly normal life."

Jake and I exchange looks again, and I can tell we're thinking the same thing: *Yeah, right, whatever "normal" is.*

Mom sees the look and continues. "It's really important for people to understand that Cody is not a bad person. And it's really, really important for you guys to forgive him."

Well, yeah. I flash back to Cody in the cafeteria, wired with bombs, how deadly serious he was, yet how young and scared and all alone he was.

"I know, Mom. I already have." I avoid Jake's eyes. He probably has more to forgive than I do.

"And," she glances at Jake, "you need to forgive yourself for being human, and for not knowing everything, because no one can know everything."

But what about me? I did know everything.

Tears run silently down my face and I wipe them away with the back of my hand. Mom passes me a tissue and says, "It's okay, it'll be okay. I'm just sorry you kids had to be a part of this...sorry you have to learn about this side of life when you're still so young."

She takes a deep breath and dries her eyes. "Cody is lucky. He has a lot of wonderful, capable people around him—grownups—who can help him. You guys are still just kids, even though you may not think so. The best way to help Cody is to be happy with yourselves and to live your lives."

We drive silently until we're almost back at school.

"Mom, can I just go home?" I just want to crawl into my bed, pull the covers up over my head and sleep 'til I'm ninety.

She looks thoughtfully at me in the rearview mirror and I'm sure she'll say yes.

"No. You need to go back to school, get back into your normal routine, and be with your friends."

What!?   That sucks.   "But Mom…" Even I can hear the pathetic whine in my voice.

"Absolutely not."

"Whatever." I shrug, sigh and gaze out the window. I feel Jake's warm hand on mine and I hold it cautiously, looking at him searchingly. He smiles at me, and we hold hands all the way back to school.

Chapter Forty-Five

The halls are buzzing with gossip as Jake and I walk to our next class.

"So how many bombs did he have—?"

"Like a hundred—"

"Where'd he get all that shit anyway—?"

"I heard he robbed a hardware store—"

"Well, he really screwed up Homecoming—"

"Nah, it's been rescheduled for this Saturday—"

"Who'd ever have thought that Cody of all people—"

"I knew, man, I knew he was emo—"

"Oh bullshit, you did not—"

"So is he, like, in the looney bin now?"

"Yeah, well, he was also arrested for attempted murder—"

"Yeah, he oughta be in jail—"

"He won't go to jail, he'll get off on insanity—"

"I heard they had to carry him outa here kicking and screaming, and they gave him some kinda elephant tranquilizer—"

That's it. I turn around and face them. "What's the matter with y'all anyway? 'Emo' and 'elephant tranquilizer,' my ass. Do you even listen to yourselves? Would you make fun of someone with cancer? Or diabetes? Or a broken leg?"

They're all quiet, just looking at me, and I should probably stop now, but I'm just getting warmed up. Jake is standing next to me, looking at me with pride and amazement.

"'Cause that's what Cody is. Sick and wounded. He needs help, just like you would if you had some kind of disease or a broken bone." I'm panting now, raging at them, and they're just staring at me with their mouths open. "I'm ashamed of all y'all! You're the ones who are emo!"

I turn on my heel to stomp away, as the silence grows deeper and longer, when I hear someone say, "Yeah! No shit!"

And then there are other voices from the crowd.

"Yeah, man, we should be feeling sorry for him."

"Yeah, who the hell are you to diss him?"

"Yeah, who are you to diss anyone? Are you so perfect?"

"Why are you ragging on Flye?"

"Yeah, like, didn't she, like, save the school?"

"Yeah, she saved all our asses man."

And then someone in the back starts chanting, "Flye is fly! Flye is fly!" No one really takes it up, but it feels good anyway and, while the Belles and the Jokes aren't joining in, they are looking at me with respect. Cammie and Maddie are actually kind of smiling at me. *The Dog Days Are Over.* Absolutely. Off to the side and in the back of the group, I see Mr. Lester smile at me in pride and tip his cap.

Chapter Forty-Six

Jake and I hang out at my locker after school, getting our stuff together to leave. "So now what're we supposed to do? Act like nothing happened?"

"Yeah, it's just so surreal," I say. "I mean, yeah, I guess, but I don't know how."

"Yeah, well, I guess we could go hang at my house, check on the tomato plants..." He trails off. This feels too real. And I know we're both thinking the same thing, how it was Cody's idea, and how it was just a way for him to get his hands on fertilizer for the bombs. It's clear to us both: we can't possibly act like nothing happened. Not ever.

Jenn jogs over to us saying, "Hey, wanna go to the cookie store?" We glance at each other like, *"Seriously?"*

"Y'all okay?"

Define "okay." Katie and Taylor have joined Jenn, and I look at them, so young and innocent, untouched by the world and all the good and bad that it holds. The whole thing with Cody was scary and exciting for them, but they're already past it, on to something new. I was like that just a few days ago. But not now. I don't feel innocent anymore. I think of that Joni Mitchell song, *Both Sides Now.*

> *"I've looked at life from both sides now,*
> *from win and lose, but still somehow;*
> *it's life's illusion I recall;*
> *I really don't know life at all."*

When your innocence goes, does that mean your childhood is gone, too? I don't know. I still feel like a kid, even though I've dealt with things that would stymie most adults. I still am a kid, technically anyway. Maybe it's a choice. Maybe that's all I have to do—choose to still be young and happy and carefree, with my whole life ahead of me. Just because I didn't feel like that on Friday, and just because I didn't feel like that a nanosecond ago, it doesn't mean I can't feel that way right now.

I look at Jake, and he's waiting for my answer. His eyes are bright and clear, and he's looking at me with so much hope and maybe something else, too.

I laugh just because it feels good. "Yeah sure. I just have to check on something in the English room."

"We'll wait for you outside," Katie says.

"Just hurry up! I'm starving!" Taylor yelps over her shoulder, already halfway out the door.

The basement is cool and silent as I walk towards the Box. I've told myself I'm over it, but I just have to see it one more time. I walk past the clutter of desks, move the white board as I've done so many times before and...

It's not there. The Box is gone. There's no door, no nothing, just a smooth, white wall. I touch the wall experimentally, waiting for the colors to glow, but nothing happens. I move my hand, both hands, and then both of my arms, pressing them frantically across the wall, waiting for something, anything. Nothing.

It's like the Box was never there. Did I imagine it? All those secrets, all the lies, all the plans, all the fears?

A small sound from my right startles me, and jumping away, I see Mr. Lester. His warm, brown eyes shine against his dark, brown skin.

"Did you lose something, Little Flye Girl?"

I stare at him for a moment, remembering all the times he's seemed to just appear and disappear; all the times I've seen him standing by the basement steps like he was waiting for me; all the times he's helped me and Jake and Cody and everyone else just try to survive the confusion and turmoil of high school. A sense of knowing, like an unspoken agreement, passes silently between us, and we smile as if we have a shared secret.

"No. I guess not."

He smiles, tips his cap and is gone. I walk up the stairs and out the front door to join my friends.

Acknowledgments

My main feeling as I complete *Flye on the Wall* is gratitude. I'm grateful for the support, encouragement, and faith I received from so many incredible people.

I wish to thank all the wonderful people at Kingman Row Entertainment for their belief in *Flye on the Wall* and their commitment to giving this story a voice.

To James Serpento, my publisher, for being the kind, generous, creative person he is; for laughing at all the right places when he first read the book and for not being able to put it down once he started it, and for taking a chance on an unknown writer with a lifetlong dream that was begging to be fulfilled.

To Madhu Koduvalli, my fabulous editor, for her resourceful and patient work with me, for knowing exactly how to combine positive feedback with constructive criticism. In my experience, that is a rare talent indeed. *Flye* would never have come to fruition without her.

To Colin Lacy, for his patient and painstaking line editing, allowing the book to be the very best it can be.

To Meghan Vosberg, my extraordinary agent, who saw the promise and potential in *Flye* and never gave up. Thank you for everything you do for me.

To Erin Tracy, cover designer, whose creativity and insight into Flye's character produced a compelling and beautiful book cover for *Flye on the Wall.*

To the Piedmont Children's Writers, a wonderful group of women who accepted me immediately and gave me direct and honest feedback during my writing process: thank you, ladies, so much.

To Katie, Jessica, and Sarah, all thirteen at the time, who were the first people I shared my original ideas with, the first to encourage me to write this book and the first to read the initial draft. Their enthusiasm, excitement and rigorous honesty in giving me feedback gave me the courage to keep moving forward. These young women will always be in my thoughts and close to my heart.

To all of the students I have taught to write, brainstormed with, conferred with, helped with the editing process, suffered through countless rewrites with, laughed, cried and torn out our hair together to get their story just right: I hope I have given you as much as you have given me.

To all of the families of the victims and survivors of the Columbine High School shootings, including the families of Eric Harris and Dylan Klebold: the grief, frantic fear and disbelief of April 20, 1999 will always live in my memory and my heart. Trite and clichéd as this is, it truly does take a village to raise a child. My deepest wish is that everyone who reads this book will be more aware and sensitive to anyone they think is in trouble and will help that person before it's too late.

To my family and extended family of friends who supported and encouraged me throughout this journey: love you guys.

To Brian and Alberto for your enthusiastic support and the joy you have both brought into my life.

To Ryan, the best son ever: I am in awe of your creativity, intellect and sheer kindness as you make your way in the world. You are the greatest teacher I've ever had. I want to be just like you when I grow up.

To Tom, my husband and my best friend, who believed in me when I didn't, who fed horses, chickens, fish, cats, and dogs, cleaned the barn, the chicken house and our house, cooked, ran errands and worked twelve-hour days at your "real" job, just so I could write this book. I love you. Always have. Always will.

About the Author

Mariah Burne is a former English teacher and a freelance writer. Her work has appeared in *Colorado Woman News* and *SCBWI Carolinas*, as well as other publications. She is a former reporter/photographer for *The Southwest Denver Herald Dispatch* and is a member of the Society of Children's Books Writers and Illustrators. She has a M.A. in Gifted Education from the University of Denver, with a concentration in creative writing. She lives in the Blue Ridge Mountains of North Carolina with her husband and their menagerie of animals. *Flye on the Wall* is her first novel.